Other books by

A Gentleman's Affair (published

"…an *excellent* book, well-written and hard to put down."

"…witty and warm, taking us on a journey of Donovan's self discovery. You will be rooting for the sexy Donovan Hart, wanting him to find his *il mio per sempre*."

"…characters the reader will care about, and moments to which everyone will relate. Donovan's dry wit had me laughing in one paragraph, his vulnerability had me crying in the next. It is a roller coaster ride with an ending that left me speechless and dying for more…"

* * * * * *

A Gentleman's Secret (published December, 2013)

"I have laughed, shouted and cried with these characters and taken them to my heart."

"…a perfect sequel…full of humor, heartache, drama, danger, and a little suspense. I don't think I will ever get enough of the confident, sexy Donovan Hart."

"I simply *love* this author's style!"

* * * * * *

A Gentleman's Memoir (published August, 2014)

"...like a refreshing drink of sparkling water on an insufferably hot day, or a hot toddy on a cold winter's night, AJ's voice as an author speaks to me...his characters are beloved friends."

"This was a perfect peek into Donovan Hart's past. All questions answered, and yet...I still want more! I've honestly never read such fun-loving, incredibly sexy books. He draws you in and seduces you with every page, and let me tell you, AJ Linn doesn't disappoint!"

"Before I had finished the first chapter I was crying, moments later I was laughing, and throughout the whole story I was fanning my face. Yes, he really brought the heat in this one. WHEW! Did he ever!"

A Gentleman's Fate

A Gentleman's Fate

by

A. J. Linn

(Vol. 4, The Gentleman's Series)

A Gentleman's Fate

ISBN: 978-0-9893767-9-2

Cover art design by Dancinee Jennings.

Dedication

I dedicate this book to all of the wonderful people who have been with me along the way. The support that I've had has been overwhelming, to say the least.

Dad, your encouragement has meant everything. Thank you.

My incredible Twitter ladies...you never cease to amaze me. Thank you, and much love to you all.

My "Team"...Scarlett, Carolyn, Romina, and Dawn. What the fuck would I do without you? Thank you, thank you, thank you, for all that you do. It still blows my mind.

Robin G-B. You have cheered me on since day one. Thank you for always having a kind word to say about these funny books. Your support has meant a lot.

Patrice (Yes, she is real) Thank you for being you, the inspiration behind my favorite character. (She is exactly like that in real life, except that I can't get her to call me sire)

Dee...Thank you for a great cover, and for hopping on the crazy train. Welcome aboard.
Dancinee Jennings on twitter @Dancinee
Website: designsbydancinee.com (Freelance Web Design, Graphic Designer)

Without the help and support of all of you, none of this would be possible. Don't think for a minute that I don't realize and appreciate that.

I hope that I have written a book that will make you laugh, cry, and hate me for fucking with your head. That would make me extremely happy...

Until we meet again...

Much love, Aj

Table of Contents

Dedication
Prologue
Chapter One
Chapter Two
Chapter Three
Chapter Four
Chapter Five
Chapter Six
Chapter Seven
Chapter Eight
Chapter Nine
Chapter Ten
Chapter Eleven
Chapter Twelve
Chapter Thirteen
Chapter Fourteen
Epilogue
Seven Months Later...
A Note From The Author

"Time is very slow for those who wait,
very fast for those who are scared,
very long for those who lament,
very short for those who celebrate.
But for those who love, time is eternal."

~William Shakespeare

8

Prologue

...To my loving wife

Donovan

My beautiful wife,
I'm writing you this letter while you are asleep in the next room. Tomorrow the big secret will be revealed, and you will finally be my wife. I won't lie, baby, I'm nervous. This will be the biggest day of our lives, and the beginning of our forever.
I promise to...

Fuck. I crumple up the paper and toss it into the wastebasket. I've never been good at writing romantic letters, so it comes as no surprise that this, my tenth attempt, sucks just as bad as all the others.

Maybe I'll try a different approach this time...

To my hot wife,
Thank you for finally marrying me, let's fuck.

I shake my head at what a loser I am as I toss that piece of paper into the trash as well. Scarlett has a sense of humor, but...

To my beautiful new wife,
Roses are red, violets are blue,
I'm a shitty writer, good thing I'm rich.

No more of that, I give up. I rub my eyes as I get up from the desk to go check on my bride-to-be.

Sound asleep.

I want to wake her up because I'm bored out of my mind. My poor girl is wrecked from a day of driving and exploring, so, being the nice guy that I am, I let her sleep. I should try to write that damn letter, but decide to open a bottle of wine instead.

On second thought...

I set the bottle down and walk back into the bedroom, and after removing my clothes, climb into bed with my girl.

"Donovan, I'm sleeping," Scarlett says, pushing my hand away from her breast.

"Enough sleeping," I say, slipping my hand into her silk panties.

"Donovan..." she says, still protesting, but not removing my hand this time.

"Scarlett..." I slip a finger inside of her, then another, feeling the warm wetness envelope my happy digits.

But the protesting quickly stops. She closes her eyes as her head sinks down into the pillow, and her legs fall open, allowing me easy access. Her hips begin to writhe as she takes fistfuls of sheets into her hands, allowing the pleasure of my fingers to take her on a euphoric ride. Her body begins to quiver, her moans grow louder.

Her fingers are in my hair now, and she grabs fistfuls and holds on tight just as an earth-shattering orgasm rips through her body.

Pause for passionate kissing and shit-eating grins of pleasure.

She removes my hand, and after sliding off her silk panties, pushes me onto my back, climbs aboard, and takes control.

One

...and for the change in your pocket I will tell you your destino.

Old gypsy woman

14

I will never forget my first trip to Italy, or my first gondola ride. I was just a kid at the time, but everything about Italy was exciting. The scent of garlic, pizza, and bread baking spilled into the streets from every restaurant and bakery. The language, the hand gestures, the crowds. I found it all fascinating. Venice was always a favorite spot of my mother's. Magico, she called it. *The place where magic happens.*

The first time my parents brought me here, the streets were flooded as they often were in Venice. The water rose so high that it soaked my shoes and socks completely. But that didn't bother me, and my parents spent more time dragging me out of puddles than anything else.

I suppose that's why bringing Scarlett here has a special meaning for me. I want her to love it as much as I do...as much as my mother did.

After a long day of doing the tourist thing, we are back in the room changing for dinner, and unbeknownst to her...a special surprise that I've been working on to follow.

"Donovan, will you at least give me a little hint so I know what to wear?" she asks while looking over the few dresses she packed.

"Whatever you choose will be perfect, babygirl. Just get dressed."

"You just don't get it. Wardrobe is everything to a girl." she says, as she removes her clothes, tossing them on the bed.

"No, I get it," I reply, laughing. "But, we have reservations so pick a dress, or go naked. I really don't care."

"Oh, you'd love that wouldn't you? Fine, I'm game," she teases, slipping into a pair of heels. "Okay, is this good?" she asks while doing a twirl in front of me.

"No complaints here, baby, but you just might get arrested if you go out like that," I reply with a smirk as I slide my hands around her waist, pulling her hard against me.

"I thought we had reservations," she says playfully as she tries to pull away.

"Mhmm, dinner can wait," I say, quickly unzipping then dropping my pants, thrusting my cock deep inside of her before she can protest any further.

"You're so bad, baby," she whispers in between moans.

"I can stop…" I reply, with no intention of stopping. Pulling out for a nanosecond, I spin her around and take her from behind, as she anchors herself on the edge of the bed.

"Never...mmm, never stop," she says, breathless.

We make our reservation, barely, at Ristorante Da Ivo, dining on Insalata Caprese and Penne all'arrabbiata, before we head to the canals.

"You were quiet during dinner, Donovan. What's wrong?" she asks as we leave the restaurant.

"Nothing, baby girl. I was just enjoying the food," I reply, shooting her a wink.

"I know, it was good...I think I gained ten pounds!" she says, laughing, rubbing her belly.

"Italy will do that to you," I say.

"It's so beautiful here, baby. Thank you for this amazing trip."

"I'm glad you think so, because I'd like to buy us a home here."

"Really? Here? In Venice?"

"Yes. What do you think about that?"

"You mean to live?" she asks, her brow suddenly furrowed.

"A vacation home for now, but I'd like to retire here someday."

"I could see that, sure."

"Good, we'll take a look around tomorrow," I reply with a nod.

"Tomorrow? So soon?"

Her eyes widen as she takes a long look around the area, and it's as if she's trying to picture herself actually living here. She frowns.

"Is something wrong?" I ask.

"No, I'm fine. Just a little overwhelmed by all of this, I guess."

That's the last thing I wanted to hear right now, and it's making me second-guess what is about to take place. Just when I think I have this girl figured out, she throws me another curve ball.

"It's just a vacation home. I don't understand what is so overwhelming about that."

"I don't either," she replies, forcing a smile. "I love the idea."

"Why don't we just go back to the room? We've had a full day, and we can do this another time."

"No! I'm dying to see this big surprise, Donovan. I'm fine, I promise!"

And, I know that she's not. Nothing has been the same since the Ricardo incident, and I'm not sure now if it ever will be. The timing just isn't right for this...not yet. I'm not sure how to go about canceling this, the gondolier and the priest are waiting, and I don't have Patrice here to make calls for me.

"Donovan? Are you okay?"

"You confuse me, Scarlett. It's always two steps forward and thirty steps back with you. Just when I think that we're back in a forward position, you drag me right back to square one."

"That's not true, baby. I love you so much, and I want to spend the rest of my life with you. You have to know that by now."

"Just five minutes ago you were overwhelmed at the thought of a vacation home here. Just make up your mind for god's sake, Scarlett."

"It's made up, I made it up a long time ago. I'm sorry I freaked out a little, I'm not used to all of this."

"All of this?" I ask.

"Yes, all of this. The romance, this vacation, the shopping trips. Buying a house here. It's a lot."

"It's called a relationship, planning a future."

"I know, but I'm allowed to get scared, Donovan. I'm not perfect like you."

"Perfect?" I reply, laughing. "I'm far from perfect, babygirl. Why don't we just go back to the hotel. I'm not really up for this shit right now."

"No, stop it. I want my surprise," she says, pleading.

"It isn't the right time, I see that now," I reply shaking my head.

"Whatever it is, I'm sure I'll love it. Now, come on, let's go." She grabs my hand and starts pulling me in the opposite direction of the canals. And, knowing now that this is a really bad idea, I lead her towards the hotel.

"What are you doing?" she asks, frowning, stopping in the middle of the cobblestone road.

"Scarlett, not now. Let's just go back to the room, and we'll discuss this later."

"No." She sighs. "Just show me, please."

As much as I don't want to, I concede, and we walk in the direction of the canals. Is it just bad timing, or am I doing all of this for the wrong girl?

We arrive at the dock, and before us is the hard-not-to-miss gondola, filled with red roses and surrounded by dozens of tiny white flickering votives. The priest and the gondolier are standing by, making the big surprise even more obvious with their shit-eating grins. It quickly becomes apparent to Scarlett what's happening, and she doesn't say a word. She just stands there, stunned, speechless, and horrified.

"Come aboard, happy couple!" the gondolier says, attempting an American accent, not overshadowing his thick Italian one. "We have-a da champagne on ice for da celebration of this most joyous of occasions!"

"The celebration? Donovan? What's going on?" she asks, not taking her eyes off of the priest. "What is this?"

"This, Scarlett, is me trying to marry you. The romantic shit that you hate, remember?"

"Donovan?" A confused, terrified look sweeps across her face.

"What do you want me to say, Scarlett? I foolishly thought you actually wanted to get married this time. And correct me if I'm wrong, but you did say that you wanted to marry me."

"No, I do...but...I'm sorry. I...I can't. Not like this, I'm not ready," she says as tears begin streaming down her cheeks. "I'm so sorry, Donovan."

And off she goes like a defective bride, leaving me standing here, yet again, feeling like an asshole.

I pay off the gondolier and the priest, apologizing profusely.

Not wanting to go back to the room, I walk the streets of Venice for awhile. I don't want to hear her excuses, deal with her crying, much less see her face.

Up ahead, tucked away in a small enclave near a run-down, closed bistro, there is an old gypsy woman draped in orange and purple scarves calling me over. For the change in my pocket -she explains- she will tell me my *destino*. Tempting, but my fate is a never-ending mess of disappointment these days, so I toss some cash into her bucket and walk on by.

After about an hour of aimless wandering, I end up back at our hotel, and am not surprised to find that Scarlett, and her suitcase are both gone. Of course, she left a note. She's good at leaving notes when she leaves me.

Without looking at a single word on the paper, I crumple it up and toss it into the nearby waste basket. Nothing she can say will fix it this time, and I won't be going after her. This girl has done enough damage to last me a lifetime, and it's time to walk away and not look back.

Destino.

Two

...I don't want to be bothered, no matter what's on fire.

D.H.

"Good morning, sire, it's good to have you back. How was Venice?" Patrice asks as I fly past her desk, walking straight into my office, slamming the door behind me.

But that doesn't stop her. She barges in with hot coffee, making herself comfortable in the black leather chair near my desk. "Okay, spill it. What's going on?"

"Not now, Patrice," I reply dismissively, switching on my computer.

In a daze, my eyes are fixed on the blank screen. I'm trying to avoid the inevitable conversation, and trying even harder to ignore her. She sets the cup down on my desk, softening her voice to almost a whisper, asking once again, "Donovan, what's going on?"

"Don't you have work to do?" I snap.

"Yes sir, I suppose I do," she snaps back defensively as she gets up from her chair, mumbling the word *asshole* under her breath as she heads towards the door.

"I heard that," I respond, somehow managing to muster up a slight chuckle. "I apologize, alright? Sit back down."

"Accepted. Now, are you gonna tell me what's got you in such a pissy mood?"

"In a nutshell...she did it again."

"She? She who? Scarlett?"

"Yes, Scarlett."

And there it is. The look that I was trying so hard to avoid. The poor-Donnie, sad-eyed, frowny-faced look that I know I'll get every single time that I tell this fucking story. Perhaps I can just handle this in one fell swoop, and have Patrice send out a mass memo describing the details of the nightmare-in-Venice, fucking-kill-me-now debacle.

"I don't get it, Donovan. She was the one that propo...."

"Please, don't even say it. I really don't want to get into this right now. Alright?"

"Sure, okay, Donnie. Can I do anything for you?"

She gets up again to leave, but pauses twice before reaching the door. I can see that she's searching for the right thing to say. Something...*anything*...to lighten the mood, to cheer me up, to lessen the blow of what Scarlett has done, now twice...as if anything could. But I just want her to leave.

"You know she loves you, right? Do you want me to talk to her? I'm sure I can..."

I interrupt before she can say anything else. "Not another goddamn word about it, understand? Now, I have work to do."

"Fine, for now. But you'll have to talk about it at some point, you know."

I continue to stare at the still-blank computer screen, waving her away.

Defeated, for now, at last she leaves, closing the door behind her.

The clock on the wall seems to be ticking slower than usual. I've been here for three hours, and am finding it impossible to concentrate, especially with my cell going off every ten minutes with calls and text messages from Scarlett. I'm not ready to talk to her, and to be honest, I don't know if I ever will be. I don't know if I even care at this point. Although I'm slightly curious, I really have no idea what we have to talk about anymore.

I need to get out of this hotel and clear my head. I knew coming here straight from the airport was probably a mistake, but it seemed like a good idea at the time. Better than sitting in that penthouse, alone, with nothing but the all-too-fresh memories of yet another Scarlett-related nightmare to keep me company.

Placing my cell phone in the top drawer of my desk, I change out of my monkey suit and into the spare set of clothes that I keep in the closet of my office. Stopping by Patrice's desk on my way out, I let her know that I'm leaving for the rest of the day, and that I don't want to be bothered, by anyone...no matter what's on fire.

"Are you okay?" she asks, still pushing, hoping for some sort of verbal spillage on the details of my Venetian vacation.

"No, but I will be."

28

Three

...Don't be an ass, Donovan, eat your cookie.

P.A.

30

I don't know why I expected to wake up this morning feeling any better about what happened with Scarlett in Venice...it has only been a couple of days. I decide it's time to face the voicemails and the countless text messages from her that flood my cell phone.

Donovan, I'm sorry. Please talk to me.

Baby, answer your phone. Let me explain.

Why won't you answer your phone? Come on, Donovan. I'm really sorry.

Call me back.

Please stop ignoring me. We have to talk about what happened.

Thirty-nine text messages, all the same. A few dozen voicemails...more of the same.

Does true love really conquer all? No, true love doesn't pull the same shit twice. I forgave her once for this, I don't have it in me to do it again.

Delete, delete, delete.

A productive morning at the office proved to be just what I needed, for now. But, I think a night at The Underground is much needed, for later...much needed. While wrapping up a business call, Patrice pops her head in to remind me that I'm having lunch with Dad and need to go.

I arrive at the restaurant and join my dad, who is seated at a table outside on the deck. We order, and catch up briefly, but I sense that this is more than a casual lunch. Dad seems nervous, uncomfortable.

"Donovan, I have something to tell you," he begins, shifting nervously in his chair. "It's in regards to the hotel."

"Alright, what is it?"

"Well, as you well know, my life is finally back on track. Shari and I are doing good, and I think it's time that I get back to work."

"What does that have to do with my hotel?" I ask, confused.

"It is still my hotel, Son. I've decided that it's time to return to the hotel business, and let you off the hook. I put way too much responsibility on you after your mother died, and I…"

"Hold on just a minute, Dad. La Fuga is my hotel now. It has been for a long time."

"Technically, no," my father says as he shifts uncomfortably again in his chair.

"Technically, yes. We signed papers...do you need to see my copy?" I snap back quickly.

"Well, Son, I hate to point this out to you, but in those papers, it was clearly stated that I could regain full ownership at anytime."

"Yes, I am aware. But, you told me then that your lawyer advised you to add that, but that you would never return. Ever, I believe is the exact word that you used."

"I really am sorry, Son, but things have changed." His voice is getting louder. Restaurant loud, but louder. It's clear he's becoming aggravated, obviously my reaction wasn't what he expected.

"Things have changed? Do you mean to tell me…"

We are momentarily interrupted by the waiter who is quickly setting our plates down on the table without a word, giving us both a second to calm down.

"You can't be serious, Dad! You just walked away from the hotel when Mom died. You walked away from everything, and now you just want me to hand it back? No questions asked?"

"I wasn't actually sure how you'd react...if you even care one way or the other."

This is not what I expected to hear when my dad invited me to lunch today. Nearly eight years to the day that I took over La Fuga, he thinks he can just come in and take it away? This is some serious bullshit!

"You didn't care. You walked away!"

"I did, yes, but I'm back. I have Shari now, and we can take it from here," he explains. "You never really wanted it anyway."

"No, not at first. But I turned La Fuga into the most successful hotel on the California coast. We book reservations a year, even two years, in advance, and I'm sorry to point out that when you and Mom ran it...well, you were lucky to even fill a month's worth of reservations."

"While that may be true, it is still my hotel."

"You gave it to me, Dad. Handed me the keys and never once looked back! I took that outdated, run-down hotel and made it what it is today!"

"I'm not going to fight about this with you, Son. Shari and I will take over one week from today, and of course, we hope you'll stay on as manager."

I can't help but laugh...is he serious with that? Fuck manager.

"You've got to be kidding me, Dad. Manager?" I get up, dropping the cloth napkin on top of my untouched plate of food. "Unbelievable! Fucking unbelievable!"

"Don't make a scene, Donovan. Sit back down."

"Thanks for lunch, Dad." And without another word from either of us, I leave, shaking my head in disbelief, shattered, and really fucking pissed off.

First Scarlett, and now this? It's not even Wednesday yet...

I call Patrice immediately.

"Did you know about this?" I ask, my tone harsh and accusatory.

"Whoa, calm down, Donovan! Know about what?"

"About Bruce and Shari taking back La Fuga?"

"What? Taking it back? Wait, what do you mean?" she asks, clearly in just as much shock as I was at the news.

"Yes, taking it back. As in, thanks for holding down the fort while I didn't give a shit. Now go!"

"Of course I didn't know, Donovan...I would've told you if I'd known. You have to know that!"

"I do know that, I'm sorry. I'm not thinking straight right now, Patrice."

"Where are you?" she asks.

"Driving...I don't know."

"You don't know?" she says, laughing. "Where are you going?"

"To tear down The Underground. Remove any trace of it before he sees it."

"You can't just tear down the club, Donovan. It's a club!"

"You know what? Fuck it, he can deal with it. It's not my problem anymore."

"Just meet me at my apartment in fifteen minutes." And she hangs up before I can reply.

Feeling like my world, and everything I have built over the last eight years is now all falling apart, I drive to Patrice's knowing that she, more than anyone, understands what I'm going through right now.

She's waiting at the door for me, asking first if I've eaten, pointing out how short lunch with Dad actually was, and knowing all too well how I am on an empty stomach. A grouchy asshole, to be exact...she reminds me.

Once inside, I fill her in, and together we devise a plan over grilled cheese sandwiches.

"That was good, thank you." Pushing my plate aside, and taking a chocolate chip cookie from a small plate in the center of the table, I can't help but laugh a little. "I never knew you were so domesticated, Patrice."

"Don't be an ass, Donovan. Eat your cookie."

"That was a compliment, actually. Scarlett didn't cook much."

"Yeah, about that. Are you ever going to fill me in?"

"What's the point? It won't change what happened. Besides, I need to deal with The Underground first."

"Okay, I'll drop it...for now. My lunch break is almost over...do you wanna ride back with me and we can fill everyone in on what's going on together?"

"Sounds good to me. He said a week, so first on the list is to call the construction company to deconstruct the club."

"I'm on it, Donnie. Let's go."

As we're driving, a text message comes in from Dawn. My jaw drops as I read it.

Oh fuck...

Four

...My entire life fits into a large U-Haul moving truck.

D.H.

40

When we arrive at La Fuga, Dawn is waiting by the door to fill us in. She explains that Bruce had come by to inform everyone that he'd be taking over, blah, blah, blah... but had decided to tour the hotel since he hadn't been around for quite sometime. She made every attempt to stop him from going downstairs...but failed.

"I appreciate that, Dawn. I'll handle it from here." I tell everyone to stay in the lobby, and make my way downstairs.

I find my dad standing in the center of the club looking bewildered, and by the scowl across his face, pretty pissed off.

"Dad, what do you think of my club?" All I can do is laugh here...this is not going to go well, and I might as well enjoy it.

"Is this funny to you? This...this...brothel, is it, Son?"

"No Dad, not a brothel. It's a…"

"This is a disgrace, Donovan. You have embarrassed me, and the Hart name. Is this how you honor your mother?"

"No, this is how I moved on with my life when I became an orphan."

"Orphan? I'm right here, Donovan. I didn't die."

"Yes, you did."

"That's not an excuse to turn this dream of mine and your mother's into a nightmare. I don't even recognize you anymore," he says, raising his voice. "What is this place? Tell me!"

"If you must know, it's a sex club."

"And?"

"And...I've made a lot of money with it, and made a lot of people very happy."

"I bet. Contributing to sexually transmitted diseases and perverts. This is unacceptable! Unacceptable!"

"That's right, Dad. You will think whatever you want, no matter what I say. Would you like to know where I really met…" I quickly stop myself. I will not bring Shari into this, she is innocent here. But he had better stop pushing me…

"Met who?"

"This club is for consenting adults, Dad, mostly couples. There is nothing bad going on here."

"I will burn it to the ground! You are not my son. I did not raise you to be some sort of sexual deviant."

"But I am, Dad. I'd rather be like this than like you. You lock yourself away for years, forgetting that you had a son at all. It's all yours now, so go ahead and burn it down."

Now this fire I will not be putting out. We stand in the room in complete silence for what seems like an hour...neither one of us wanting to break it. What else is there to say?

So, I leave. I go to my office to collect my personal things, and Patrice and Dawn follow me in, asking what happened.

“You couldn't hear?”

“We heard,” Patrice answers.

“Alright then. Nothing more to say.”

“I don't know what to do here, Donovan,” Dawn says.

“Dawn, you have a job here for however long you want one. Everyone does. This was my doing, and it doesn't affect you.”

“Of course it affects us. This is our place, and it’s nothing without you here.”

“Listen, I am going to Pisa, and whoever wishes to join me there has a job.”

“Donovan, just talk to your dad. I'm sure when he calms down he’ll listen,” Patrice adds.

“No, I am done talking. Please send out a mass email explaining everything to all of the employees, and I’ll call Jared, Adam, and Matt tonight.”

“I will, sire” Patrice replies with tears in her eyes.

“No need for that. This is a good thing...it’s time for a fresh start.”

“So I can come too, Donovan?” Dawn asks.

“Pack your bags, Dawn,” I reply with a wink.

Bruce comes back upstairs to the lobby where we are congregating, and announces that he'll be taking over immediately, closing the hotel until further notice for renovations. Everyone stands there dumbfounded and speechless. An uncomfortable silence fills the lobby as Patrice and I exchange nods, and I walk out, leaving La Fuga behind me without a word.

The end of an era, perhaps? But on to new beginnings. Pisa won't know what hit it, but Las Vegas is known as Sin City, so I think we'll fit in just fine there.

My entire life fits into a large U Haul moving truck. Packed and ready to start my new adventure, the penthouse is empty, and although bittersweet, I feel good about this. And no, Bruce and I still haven't spoken since the day at The Underground.

Patrice, who has been helping out at Pisa already, Dawn, Lily, and Jared will all make the move with me. Reggie has a new lady, so he's staying in Malibu for now. Matt and Adam are both on the fence, so will be staying behind as well.

This mess has had me so occupied that I've completely ignored all of the messages that are still coming in from Scarlett. It's been about a week now, and she is still at it. I have decided to just leave it all behind…her, Dad, La Fuga...all of it.

Time for a new chapter.

Five

...Not your daddy's brothel.

D.H.

The move was a simple one. A four-hour drive from Malibu to Las Vegas, and before I even arrived, the movers had all of my belongings brought up to my penthouse at Pisa. It already felt like home.

Patrice will be here in a few days, followed by Dawn, and Jared by the end of the week. Unfortunately, Lily overestimated Christopher's willingness to relocate, so she won't be joining us after all. It will be impossible to find a replacement that will posses her cooking skills, as she replicated my mother's recipes like no one else could. I will be forever grateful for the time she took to pass those recipes onto the chef at Fiorella's, and showing them step-by-step how to prepare each and every dish. Just another sign of how everything is changing. But, I digress…

My first order of business...finding a building to house what will become the new Underground. Pisa just doesn't have the right set-up, so it'll have to be an off-site brothel, as my dad put it. Still laughing about that one. Perhaps the new club's name should be Not Your Daddy's Brothel. Hmm...probably not.

Later that afternoon, I meet up with Cristen, an agent that was referred to me by my buddy Russ, outside of the first location on the long list of properties that we'll be looking at today for the new club.

Cristen, I am not disappointed to tell you, is one smoking hot little package. Just my type. Long golden-brown hair, green eyes, petite, angelic smile...body by design, and perfectly designed for the newly single me to get on top of. But this is business, I have to keep reminding myself.

So, when was it ever bad to mix a little business with pleasure I ask you? Scratch that. Danielle and Scarlett...need I say more?

"Mr. Hart, I presume?" She offers her delicate hand to me, and we have one of those eyes-locking, lingering-too-long, shaking-hands-too-long sort of moments. Instant connection, check. Sexual chemistry, check.

"Cristen, please call me Donovan," I reply, trying hard not to stare. "It's really nice to meet you."

"The pleasure is all mine, Donovan," she says in an extremely flirtatious voice.

"Shall we?" And with my hand placed firmly on the small of her back, we go inside location number one.

"This space has everything you requested. It's near Pisa, just two blocks off the strip, and aside from the oversized main room, includes eight smaller rooms, ample private parking around the back of the building, and a small kitchen."

"Yes, this is just what I'm looking for actually," I reply, scanning the large room envisioning a bigger, better Underground. "I'd like to see the rest before I make a decision."

"Of course," she says. "Right this way."

And she wasn't kidding, this space is everything that I wanted. Almost twice the size of The Underground, missing only a bar, which will be easy enough to add...considering the size of the place.

I envision sex swings in every corner, themed rooms, a perfect spot for the stage, and one for the bar. It needs new paint and light fixtures, but all of that is easy to change. I'm making mental notes of everything, including color schemes to be used...which I learned from working with Scarlett. Somebody kill me. I can actually see swatches in my head...I have officially lost my man card.

"This is a great space," I say. "Draw up the papers."

"Great! I wish all my clients were this easy to please," she replies, laughing.

"Yes, well, you're very good at your job, Cristen."

"Thanks, I try." I'm not sure if she's embarrassed or flirting, but her cheeks become flushed, and her voice is now softer. "I can run the papers by Pisa on Friday, if that works for you?"

"Friday works for me, thank you." We make our way towards the door, out to our cars, and say our goodbyes.

"Looking forward to it, Donovan, and thank you."

Yep, definitely flirting.

"Until then, Cristen, and it's my pleasure," I reply, shooting her a wink.

I watch...maybe gawking just a little, as she walks away. Hips swaying, cute little ass shaking, and I can't help but think...everyone says that the best way to get over someone is to get under, or in my case, on top of someone new. Actually, under still works, so does behind...but, clichés aside, I'm just not sure that using this nice girl for sex is the best approach to my situation. Am I still that guy? Maybe I am, but I don't mix business with pleasure these days...and fucking Scarlett still owns my heart. Idiot, I know.

Have I digressed lately? No? Well, I'm doing that now.

There will be no fucking of random girls, at least not today.

So, I spend the rest of the afternoon calling contractors and working on permits.

A lot has happened in such a short time that I've barely had time to catch my breath, and all work makes me a very unhappy man. I need to rectify that situation, stat.

Six

...So, Hunky...what brings you to my little shop for whores?

Brice

"Donovan, baby, wake up."

What the fuck? Squinting through heavy lids, I see her sitting next to me on my bed. Why is she here, and who the hell let her in? Time to fire my security guy.

"How the fuck did you get in?" I ask, sitting up in what was my warm bed, but she brought the cold in and ruined that.

"I have nothing to say to you, Scarlett. Just go."

"I take it you never read my letter?"

"I'm not interested in anything you have to say right now, and I wasn't then either."

"Donovan, it's complicated, and everything was moving so fast, and...I…"

"How did you even know I was here?" I ask, ignoring her whining.

"I went to see you at La Fuga and your dad told me. I'm sorry about all of that, by the way. I can't even begin to imagi…"

"Stop it! Just stop. It doesn't concern you." I get out of bed and go into the bathroom closing the door behind me.

"Baby, talk to me. Please..." she pleads through the door.

"Can I piss in privacy? And stop calling me that. I'm not your anything anymore."

"Okay, I'll wait," she insists.

"No, please don't. I have a busy day, and you need to go."

"I'm not going until you hear me out."

I walk back into the bedroom and over to my closet. She begins her explanation while I grab a pair of sweats and a t-shirt from the closet floor. Uninterested in anything that she has to say, I tell her to be gone before I return, then leave the penthouse and head outside for a run.

Running on the sidewalk will never be the same as running along the beach, not to mention that I'll never get used to the concrete buildings that replace the shoreline as my view. Perhaps it has just hit me that I no longer live in Malibu. It's just a four-hour drive away, but right now, that doesn't exactly make me feel any better. I have to give this some time…

During my pavement-pounding run, I stumble upon a small sex shop just off the strip. Deciding to go in and check it out, I'm greeted by a tall, spiky-haired man, late thirties I'd say, who introduces himself as Brice, the owner. He actually reminds me of Slade in a lot of ways.

"Good to meet you, I'm Donovan Hart," I say as we share a firm handshake.

"Donovan Hart, owner of Pisa, Donovan Hart?"

"The one and only," I reply, laughing.

"Your hotel is fabulous, I just love, love, love it there," he says as he does some sort of sashaying, hip-swinging walk back to the counter.

"Well, thank you. I like it." Definitely reminds me of Slade.

"So, Hunky...what brings you to my little shop for whores?" He actually said that with a straight face…

"I was just passing by, and wanted to see what you carried." By the looks of it, not much. The shop is small, and most of the shelves have very few items displayed.

"Baby, we may be small but we have everything your little heart could desire. And if we don't, we'll get it for you."

"I'm looking for a few larger-scale items for a club I'm opening up just a few blocks over."

"A club? So tell me about this incredible club, Hunky..."

As he searches through a pile of books behind the counter, I assume, for a catalogue, I see Scarlett walk past the shop. I turn my attention back to Brice, and we start looking through the catalogue as I tell him about my new club.

"It sounds just fabulous," he says, listening intently. "Just what this tired old neighborhood could use."

"I've seen a lot things in this town, but never anything that I'd refer to as tired," I reply, laughing.

"Oh, it's just an expression, handsome. Loosen up."

And there it is...he winked at me.

Now, you all know that I'm a pretty open guy, but I will never get used to men flirting with me. But...time to digress. Yes?

"Oh my gawd, here you are, Donovan. I was getting worried," Scarlett says as she bursts through the shop door and hurries toward the counter.

"Brice, thank you for everything. I'll be in touch." I shake his hand and quickly turn my attention toward my stalker, Miss Montgomery.

I grab her by the arm, leaving the store. What is it with this girl? She obviously can't decide if she's coming or going. Time to handle her for once and for all.

"What is it with you? You've already made your decision to go away, so now please just stay away, for Christ's sake."

"You wouldn't read the letter or hear me out this morning, now you need to let me talk!" she insists.

"Not here. We'll do this back at my place."

I turn and begin to walk in the direction of Pisa, and she follows. This shit is becoming so redundant, and I already know what's to come. More of her insecurities, more sad stories, more empty promises. But I fear if I don't give her five minutes, she may haunt me for eternity. So, here we go...again.

“Alright, speak.”

“Jesus, Donovan. You don't have to talk to me like that.”

I walk into the kitchen to make coffee, and even though this feels like more of a Jack ‘n Coke moment, it’s too early for that, even for me.

“Are you even listening to me?”

“I'm listening.”

“Aren’t you going to offer me a cup of coffee?”

I turn to look at her, my eyes shooting daggers straight in her direction. I raise my mug in the air, and coldly reply, “No.”

“You know, I don't need this. I wanted to explain, but you're just being a dick.”

She gets up from the couch to leave, and tears start to stream down her cheeks. Unaffected, I give her a wave. “Alright.”

“I get that you're mad. I get that I did this. But, after everything, I at least deserve to be heard out!”

“After everything...I didn't deserve to be fucked with, by you, twice! Now, weren’t you leaving?”

After a few rounds of pacing on my living room floor, and finally realizing that, yes, I am pretty pissed off, she leaves.

I finish my coffee, try to get my focus back, and jump in the shower.

Forward motion, fresh start, new chapter...

Seven

...The sex rooms? Ew, no thank you!

P.A.

The large sticky note placed in the middle of my computer screen, one of many, actually, reminds me of all the things that I need to do today. Patrice and, thankfully, her organizational skills arrive later this afternoon...so after making a mental note of my notes, I remove them all, tossing them in the trash. She despises those things...says they clutter up the joint.

My appointment with Cristen to finalize the club papers is in an hour, so I head to the restaurant for a quick bite before she gets here. I've missed the smells coming from Fiorella's, and I'm reminded of my mother's recipes once again, and what a great job Lily did bringing this staff together.

Just as I'm finishing up the last of my ravioli, I hear a familiar, most-welcome voice behind me, followed by a tap on my shoulder. "Get to work, sire." Patrice says with a giggle.

I turn around and am greeted by her warm, beautiful smile, which seems to always include an underlying smirk of playfulness. I stand, pulling her into a tight embrace.

"It's about time you got here."

"Can't live without me, can you?" she says, laughing.

"I wouldn't want to try," I reply sarcastically. "Are you hungry? Join me."

"No, I'm good, thanks. How is everything going here?" she asks.

"Good. Great, actually. I need to get you filled in, but I have a meeting in a few minutes."

"Meeting?"

"Closing on a new club space."

"Oh, that's exciting. I can't wait to see it!" she says, beaming.

"Let me wrap this up and then I'll take you," I say as I get up from the table. "By the way, I had the maid service give your usual suite a freshening up this morning."

"Perfect, thanks!" she says. "I'll get settled and unpack...just let me know when you're ready to go."

"Will do." I drop a twenty on the table, and escort Patrice to the elevator. "Let me know if you need anything at all."

"Go have your meeting, I'm all set." The elevator doors close, and I head back to my office where Cristen is already waiting in the reception area.

"Cristen, I apologize if I kept you waiting." I extend my hand, then lead her into my office.

"Oh no, I was a few minutes early," she says, smiling.

"Please, have a seat." I nod, sitting down behind my desk, settling into my black leather office chair.

"Okay, everything is good to go," she says, pushing the lease across my desk. "Just sign anywhere you see a sticky note."

"And where are we with permits for the remodel?" I ask, giving the papers a thorough look before signing.

"All good. Everything you faxed over seemed fine and has been submitted. You shouldn't have any problems there."

"Very good. I'm looking forward to getting the club open as soon as possible."

"Well, if there's anything I can do, just give me a holler."

"Alright," I reply, laughing. "I just might do that."

"What did I say that was so funny?" she asks, now laughing with me.

"It's nothing." I hand her back a signed copy of the lease before standing up to show her out.

"Okay, well, it was a pleasure doing business with you, Donovan," she replies, handing me the keys to the new space.

"The pleasure was all mine, Cristen, and, I'll be sure to...holler at you soon." I give her a playful wink, and she is off.

Now, to check in on Patrice, and fill her in on my interesting week.

I knock on the door of her executive suite, and am greeted by a Patrice that I've never seen before. Short-shorts, clingy tank, and fit, tanned legs that frankly, I didn't know existed. Patrice is always dressed in barely-above-the-knee skirts, always business-like, bordering on matronly...certainly never short, never tight. While I've always found her attractive, I have never seen her in this light. Sexy, with a different kind of confidence.

"Come in, I'm almost done unpacking."

I try hard not to notice her perfect ass as she walks back to the closet. She is doing those cut-offs a favor. I need to look away...this is Patrice we are talking about here.

"Take your time. The rest of my day is free." Taking a seat on the plush chocolate-brown couch near the window, I fight the urge to stare...but am still surprised at what this woman has been keeping hidden under her business attire for all of these years.

"How was your meeting?" she asks.

"It went well...signed, sealed, and I have the keys to my new club," I say, twirling the set of keys around my finger.

"Are you excited?"

"I am, of course. I just wish that I was opening a new club under different circumstances."

"I know, but Donnie, you really need to set things right with your dad. He loves you."

"Any issues breaking the lease on your apartment?" I ask, swiftly changing the subject.

"Don't do that, don't ignore this," she says, almost scolding me.

"Scarlett came by the other day," I digress.

"No! Seriously?"

“Seriously. It was...well, interesting.”

“Tell me. What did she say?”

“Not a lot, actually. I didn't give her the chance.”

“Aren’t you the least bit curious as to why she left?”

“Nope.”

“Liar. I know you better than that.”

“So, did you have any issues breaking the lease?” I ask a second time.

“You brought her up, not me, Donovan. I know you want to talk about it.”

“At some point, perhaps. But right now, I’d rather show you the new club space.”

“You're such an asshole.”

“I know.”

“Just give me a minute to change.” She grabs a blouse and a pair of jeans, taking them into the bathroom.

“I think you look great...in that, actually.”

She pops her head out with a confused, yet intrigued look across her face, only responding with, “Really?”

“Yes, really. You should dress in that more often.”

“Very businessy, Donnie. Maybe when I quit working for you and start working the strip.”

I can hear her giggling through the closed door, and when she emerges, she chucks a balled-up towel at me. “Let's go!”

“You know, it wouldn't be a bad thing if you dressed a little less businessy, as you put it. We're in Vegas now. Break a rule or two.”

“Are we taking my car or yours?”

“We can walk, Patrice. It's close.”

“Isn't that convenient for you?”

“Yes it is,” I reply with a nod.

“Is it going to be just like The Underground?” she asks.

“It is. Just a bigger, better version.”

“And you know that I'm still not gonna hang out there, right?”

“I figured as much, but I plan to change that.”

“Not happening,” she says, laughing.

Once inside the new space, I show her around, explaining my vision. She's pretending not to be interested, but I'm not buying it. At the very least, she's intrigued.

"Hey Donnie...you should put the deejay booth in this corner, maybe on a riser just behind the new bar," she says, pointing.

"That's actually genius, Patrice. I like it. I'll talk to the contractor about it tomorrow."

"Thank you, sire. With my input, this place will be amazing."

"Well, let's not get carried away here. One great idea does not a club make."

"That didn't even make sense, you idiot," she says, howling with laughter.

"It made perfect sense. And by the way, clean out your locker, smartass."

"Not again!" She laughs, I laugh. Together we are a two-man/woman comedy team, except for the fact that no one would pay us a penny to perform this shit...

Time to digress…

"Would you like to see the rooms?" I ask.

"The sex rooms? Ew! No thank you!" she replies, making a strange sour-puss face.

"Okay, they aren't sex rooms yet, and you need to lighten the fuck up, girl."

"Girl?" she replies laughing, again.

"You are a girl, right?"

"Last time I checked."

"Want me to double-check for you?"

"Donnie, knock that crap off. I'm not one of your girls!"

"No, that's not what I meant...I just meant to say… Fuck it. Never-mind."

"So, you said there was a kitchen?"

"I did. Right this way, girl."

After an uncomfortable pause, we quickly get back to the business at hand. She explains why my ideas for paint, and thoughts on color schemes are all wrong, and offers her advice on the proper way to choose colors for depth and pop. I don't know about all of that, I'm not sure what needs to pop, but I give her full authority on all things color-related.

"So, you said that you picked a name?"

"I did."

"Okay…?"

"Bruce's Las Vegas Bordello," I say convincingly.

"Donovan, that's not even funny."

"I think it's extremely funny, actually."

"And the real name?"

"Above Ground. Get it? Because this one is above ground, and the other one is…"

"I get it, jeez! Stop messing around..." she says, laughing.

"Okay, I will stop messing around." I nod.

"I'm leaving," she says playfully as she heads towards the door.

"Destino, Patrice. I am naming it *Destino*."

"Um, okay. Why?"

"I know it isn't your typical adult club name…"

"Because I would know," she says, shrugging her shoulders.

"Shut up. May I continue?"

"Please."

"Thank you. All of the shit that's happened...Scarlett, my dad, the club...it's all brought me here. Make sense? The fact that Pisa was already a reality just solidifies everything."

"And everything is?"

"Are you listening? Patrice...I belong in Italy, and all of this is just a means to that end."

"Okay, I wasn't expecting that, but I'm with you..."

"It makes perfect sense. I've always been closer to my mom...do you see where I am going here? At all?"

"I do...I get it, Donnie."

"I'm going to get back to my roots, Patrice. Hence, why I built this hotel. I just didn't know the whole picture at the time."

"You're such a mama's boy," she says, teasing me still.

"Yes ma'am. Absolutely." I nod in full agreement.

"I just don't see how the club fits into this picture."

"The club is for fun, Patrice. Just because I have this long-term goal doesn't change who I am...what I like to do…"

"Whoa! Stop right there! I don't need to know about any of that."

"Alright, let's just pretend that you've never seen any of…"

"Stop!" she repeats, scowling.

"Stop interrupting me."

"I can't," she says, holding her hands over her ears, laughing.

"So, now you're three?" I ask, shaking my head.

"Can we go now?"

"Yes, we can go now," I reply, chuckling. I remove her hands from her ears and escort her out.

"Well, that was interesting," she says, rolling her eyes.

As we approach the entrance to the hotel, ignoring her sarcasm, I ask, "Are you hungry?"

"Always," she answers.

"Let me buy you dinner...to make up for all of those visions that will be dancing through your mind tonight when you go to sleep."

"You're so disgusting, Donovan."

"I know," I reply with a smirk. "I'll meet you at Fi's in an hour. I need a shower."

"Fi's...that's cute, Donnie," she says, laughing. "I'll meet you there."

Eight

...You're beginning to sound like a twelve-step program, Patrice.

D.H.

No surprise, I am on time, and she is not. I sit at my usual table, and order a Jack 'n Coke while I wait. An hour has passed...actually it passed about fifteen minutes ago. But, if there's one thing I've learned about women, it's that they are always late...and that it's usually worth the wait.

"Sorry, Donnie. I don't want to hear it," she says as she rushes to the table.

"Hear what? I'm on Vegas time now, Patrice...we have all night. So, cheers to that." I raise my glass before taking a drink. "You look beautiful, by the way."

"A compliment? Are you feeling okay?" The waiter comes over and she orders a glass of house white then picks up a menu.

"Never better, actually, but I appreciate your concern." I nod.

"I can't remember a time when I wasn't worrying about you."

"And why is that? Why do you worry about me so much?" I ask, taking another sip.

"Because you pay me to."

"Then I think it's time for a raise," I say, raising my glass again.

"You're telling me, mister!" she replies, laughing.

"Dinner first? I would rather negotiate the terms of your pay raise on a full stomach."

"Fine, but I'm going to negotiate a huge moving bonus, so drink up!"

"My business mind is always intact, even while under the influences of alcohol and beautiful women." I shoot her a wink that we both ignore.

"Keep drinking," she says, now raising her glass for a toast. "To new beginnings, being under the influence, and to my intoxicating beauty." And she awkwardly follows that with a shoulder-shrugging, eye-rolling combo as we clink glasses.

"Are you ready to order?" I ask.

I call the waitress over, ordering two plates of the lasagna Lily has so perfectly replicated from my mother's recipe box for the restaurant, and another round of drinks. Fiorella's is packed to capacity which would, no doubt, please my mother. And *that* is how I honor her…

"Alright, Donnie. You can't escape the question any longer. Tell me what happened in Venice."

"You just aren't going to let this die, are you?"

"No, I'm not. Now spill it!"

"Patrice, if I knew, I'd tell you," I begin, shaking my head. "I had everything set up, the gondola ride at sunset, the priest...but she ran. She just left me standing there, again."

"That makes no sense. She's the one who wanted to get married again after the Ricardo thing happened."

"Yes she was," I reply, shrugging my shoulders. "I don't get it either, Patrice. The girl is clearly fucked-up in the head."

"That's not fair, Donovan. She's been through a lot in her life."

"Then she needs help, and she needs to stop leaving me at the altar. I've had enough."

"I don't blame you, but don't you at least want to hear her out?"

"No, I really don't."

"Donovan, you love this girl. Isn't she worth another chance?"

"No, she isn't. And I'm surprised that you've decided to take her side in all of this."

"No, I'm not taking her side, I just feel sorry for her."

"So do I, but I will feel sorry for her from a distance now. I am done with her."

"I'm not sure if I believe that, but if you say so."

"I say so," I reply, nodding. "Next subject, please."

"The lasagna is amazing," she says, smiling, taking another bite.

I nod in agreement.

"So, you're not talking now?"

“I'm eating.”

“You're such a jerk.”

“I know.”

Perfect timing...the staff comes over to the table with a large white sheet cake, the words, *Welcome Back, Bossman* written in red piping across the top. Just another reminder that moving here was the right decision.

“Thank you, everyone. I'm glad to be a full-time resident now, and look forward to what the future of Pisa has to bring.” I raise my glass, and give a nod to all of the smiling, eager faces of the Pisa staff.

“That was sweet of them,” Patrice says, watching as they walk away from the table.

“Yes it was,” I nod, touched by the staff's kind gesture.

“Okay, I'm going to say one last thing about this, and then I'll stop.” She takes a quick pause for sip of wine before continuing. “Getting over someone is one of the hardest things to do in life. You saw a future with her, and now that that future no longer exists. You need to stop pretending it didn't happen, deal with it...get mad, allow yourself to be hurt...then you can move forward.”

“You're beginning to sound like a twelve-step program, Patrice.”

“Because you're pretending it never happened.”

"No, I am choosing to move forward in the only way I know how."

"But…"

"No buts, Patrice. Now let me say this...the first time she left was like a sharp knife to the stomach, but I survived. This time, I just should have known better, hence, much easier to move on. Capisce?"

"Capisce. I get it." She nods.

"I'm fine, but will you be? You seem more upset about this than I am."

"I'm upset that she did it to you again."

"Think about it this way. She didn't wait to leave five, ten years in, wasting my life after punching out a couple of kids, right? For that, I thank her."

"Makes sense, but I know you, and I know deep down you're hurt."

"I'm not made of steel, Patrice. It sucks, but now it's time to move on."

"Okay, you're right." She raises her glass, again. "To moving forward."

"Didn't we already toast to this?"

"Can't you ever just let me have a moment of greatness?"

"Drink your wine."

So we drink, we laugh, and...decide to go dancing. Now I know she is drunk. We walk across the street to a small club to continue our dual-celebratory evening.

Nine

...Her? I'm a HER now?

S.M.

"Why am I at your penthouses? It's really dark in here," a tipsy Patrice says, slurring.

"Just one penthouse, and you're here because you lost your keycard," I reply, as I lead her to my room then over to the bed, turning on a small lamp on the nightstand.

"I can't sleep here, lemme go find my key."

"I already called down to reception, and a new key will be here in a few minutes."

"Oh, Donnie, you're so smart. I've always liked that about you."

I can't help but laugh at how agreeable she is after a few drinks. "I'm making some coffee."

"No...I want wine!" she says, whining. "I can't believe that I'm on your bed."

"No more wine for you," I reply, laughing.

"You're supposed to be Mr. Party Guy," she says, adding air quotes. "The life of the party. Now, bring me a glass of wine!"

"All out." I sit down on the bed next to her, handing her a hot cup of strong black coffee. "Drink this."

"So, no wine?" she asks, pouting a she takes the cup.

"Just drink your coffee," I reply, laughing, hearing a knock on the door. "That's probably your key. Drink."

I answer the door, and much to my surprise and disappointment, find a stunned Scarlett standing there, tears in her eyes. "You're sleeping with Patrice now? I can hear her yelling all the way down the hall."

"What do you want, Scarlett?" I ask, ignoring her accusation.

"Scarlett? Where is she? Let me talk to her!" Patrice says, stumbling her way through the room, joining us at the door.

"Go back to your coffee," I tell Patrice. "I can handle her."

"Her? I'm a HER now?" Scarlett asks, turning on the full-blown water works.

"No, I'm talking," Patrice says as she shoves me out of the way. "Scarlett...little Miss Scarlett. You just might be the stupidest girl in the world, treating my friend like that. You don't deserve to talk to him, you don't deserve to see him."

"You're right, Patrice, but he needs to hear me out, and you are my friend, too, so please stay out of it."

"No, I'm not staying out of it, and you need to stay away from him. He's wonderful, and amazing, and...wonderful. You don't just hurt a guy like him even once, but no, Miss Scarlett does it twice."

"You're drunk...and sleeping with my fiancé. How could you, Patrice?" Scarlett asks, still crying.

"Yep, and you have to go now, *ex*-fiancé...so, bye." Patrice waves her off, and leans against a nearby wall.

"Scarlett, just leave," I interrupt. "There isn't anything more to say, it's done."

"It's not done, and if you'd hear me out, you'd understand why…"

"No. I am done trying to understand you. Now, please just go," I say in a not-fucking-around-anymore tone.

"Donovan, stop. I'm your fiancé!"

Good god, more crying…

"Were! You *were* his fiancé, Scarlett, but you blew it! Now you heard the man, it's time for you to move along now," Patrice says, becoming more coherent.

"Alright, Patrice. I appreciate the backup, but I've got this," I say, interrupting yet again.

"Okay, Donnie. I'll be right over here if you need me." She points in the direction of my room, and back to her cup of coffee she goes.

"Goodbye Scarlett," I say, attempting to close the door, not only on her, but on our relationship.

"Donovan, please?" she pleads.

"I'm not going to ask you again. Leave or I will have security escort you out."

"Security?" she asks. "You'd actually call security on me? Who are you? I don't even know you anymore."

"Well, one thing I am not, is your fiancé. Now, for the last time...leave!"

And after standing there for thirty seconds too long, dumbfounded...although I don't understand why...with tears running down her cheeks, and red, swollen eyes, she finally leaves. Hopefully this time for good.

"Donnie, you know what?" Patrice calls out as I close the door.

"What, Patrice?"

"She kinda reminds me of Danielle," she says, letting out a cute snort-laugh combo.

But she does have a point. This has all been reminiscent of the cheating whore, although Scarlett didn't cheat...as far as I know, and was never after my money.

"A little bit, yes," I reply, laughing as I walk back into the room only to find a passed-out-cold Patrice. I cover her with a blanket, and set myself up on the couch.

The next morning, a knock on the door wakes me from a somewhat comatose state of slumber, and the first thing I think is, that had better not be Scarlett. The time on the clock reads ten-thirty, and I'm surprised to find Patrice still asleep in my bed. I close the door to the bedroom, and walk, still half-asleep, to see who is behind door number one this time.

"Dad? What are you doing here?" I ask, shocked to see him in Las Vegas.

"Not a very warm welcome, Son...not that I expected one."

"Just surprised to see you here," I say, stepping away from the door. "Come in."

"Do you have a minute?" he asks as he follows me into the living room. "I have something that I need to say to you." He removes his jacket, tossing it over the arm of the couch before sitting down.

"If it involves you dragging me through the shit again regarding The Underground, then no." I sit down in the chair on the other side of the room, but suspect this won't take long.

"No, I won't be dragging you through the shit again," he replies. "Shari told me everything about how the two of you really met, and although I am still against all of...that, I understand a bit more now."

"Was that an apology?" I ask, raising my brow.

"This isn't easy for me, Son. How about you give your old man a break?"

"Apologizing has never been easy for you, has it?"

"Was there something else that I should be apologizing for?" he asks.

"No, Dad, and I accept your apology. Was that all?"

"No, actually. I would like for you to come back to La Fuga and be my partner. I was wrong to ask you to step down to manager after all that you've done...for the hotel, and yes, for me...since your mother passed."

"Yes, that was wrong, and thank you for that, but I am staying in Las Vegas."

"Think carefully about your decision, Son. I won't make this offer again."

"Everything on your terms, right, Dad?" I reply, shaking my head. "My decision stands, I will be staying here. Permanently."

"Well, I am sorry to hear that," he says, looking around my large penthouse, an extremely upgraded version from the one that I spent years living in at La Fuga.

"Pisa is doing well then?" he asks.

"You sound surprised."

"No, actually I'm not surprised in the least. I always knew that you had it in you to be great. Once you stopped acting like a spoiled little shit."

"Yes, well..." I pause to laugh. "My parents made me a spoiled shit, but I grew up."

"You're right, we did spoil you. You were the light of your mother's life, and you brought her so much joy. I wasn't about to ruin that for her."

"And you never cross an Italian woman, right?" I say, laughing.

"Exactly, Son. And God help you if you do."

The conversation takes a turn, and we are both laughing now. Dad gets up from the couch, and making himself at home, pours a cup of coffee. I join him in the kitchen offering breakfast, and before we know it, a groggy Patrice enters the room...black makeup smudged under her eyes, yawning, and looking like last night's party girl.

"Well, good morning to you," my dad says, looking at her, confused as fuck.

"Bruce? Hi, uh, good morning." Her face turns a few dozen shades of red, and I can tell that she wants to crawl into a hole and hide right now.

"Coffee?" I ask her, smirking. "Dad, we went dancing last night, and she lost her key card, so I let her sleep here," I explain, not really knowing why I feel the need to do so.

"Patrice," my dad repeats, giving her a nod. "And this is none of my business, although I have to say that I'm not surprised."

"No, Dad, nothing happened..."

"Mhmm…" he interrupts, "I believe you."

"Alright, who wants bacon and eggs?" I ask, changing the subject quickly.

This is going to be one interesting morning...

Ten

...You kinda wanna hit on me now, huh?

Dawn

92

Day One: Patrice Hangover Watch continues. When I left her she was attempting to eat a piece of bacon, but she basically just sat there making faces at the greasy slice on her plate. Clearly being the only one that needs to actually work for a living, I left her and Dad in the penthouse and went down to my office.

Happy to report that my cell hasn't been going off yet this morning, so all is quiet on the Scarlett front for now. I know I'll need to talk to her at some point, but being that this is round two in the case of the missing bride, I'm completely uninterested in her excuses.

Hoping for a quiet, uneventful day.

And, as usual...I spoke too soon. Just as I'm settling in behind my desk, Dawn walks in, earlier than expected, and she is as loud and bubbly as always. My slight hangover is annoyed by her volume, but nonetheless, I am happy to see her face. As soon as Jared arrives, the team will be complete...well, as complete as it's going to be for now anyway.

"Dawn, good to see you. How was the move?"

"It was good, thanks! I'm super excited to be here!" she replies in a high-pitched tone.

"Good, I'm glad," I respond, with a slight chuckle. "I have a suite all ready for you on the same floor as Patrice and Jared. Would you like to see it?"

"My new home?" she asks, laughing. "Yeah, I'm totally dying to see it!"

"Your home as long as you want it, Dawn," I answer as I stand and escort her out of the office towards the elevator. "And there's no hurry to find an apartment, alright?"

"Cool, thanks. I'll probably stay here for at least three months."

"As I said, yours for as long as you want it," I say as the elevator doors open. "After you..."

I show her to the Imperial Suite, and give her a quick tour. While she is gushing about the oversized sunken tub in her bathroom, I explain about room service discounts, maid service on request only, etc.

"That's actually perfect because I don't really want someone in my room every single day," she says, smiling while checking out her closet space.

"Very good," I reply with a nod. "Keep in mind, though, that they are always available for any emergency you might have."

"Like a cleaning emergency?" she says sarcastically.

"Don't be a smartass, you know what I mean. Your things are being brought up now, and I have work to do, so if you need anything else you know where to find me."

"Thanks, boss. Uh, where's Patrice? I didn't see her at her desk."

"Patrice is having breakfast with my dad."

"Wait, your dad's here?" she asks, surprised.

"He is. And before you ask, everything is smoothed over with him, but we'll get into that later."

"No problem," she says. "You go run your fancy hotel, and I'll be here unpacking."

"Why don't we all have dinner together?" I ask just before I leave her room.

"Okay, cool. Just tell me when and where."

"Will do. Welcome to your new home, Dawn."

I make my way down the hall to check on Patrice, knocking on her door a few times...no answer. So I take the private elevator up to the penthouse, which is also empty. I leave a message on her cell and go back down to my office.

I find my dad sitting in the reception area flipping through a magazine, but no Patrice. "Dad, have you seen Patrice?"

"No, I left her in your penthouse," he answers with a shrug.

"Hmm, alright. I can't seem to find her."

"She could be asleep or taking a shower."

"Or throwing up…" I say, laughing. "So Dad, how long are you staying?"

"I just drove out to talk to you, I'm actually leaving soon."

"Why don't you stay for dinner? Dawn just arrived, and it'll give you more time to catch up with Patrice."

"No, I think I'll get in a little gambling, then head back. Shari doesn't like to be home alone for too long."

"Why didn't you bring her?" I ask.

"She was afraid of how things might have gone, I suppose."

"Well, I can't blame her for that."

"No, certainly can't," he says, getting up, tossing the magazine on the table. "I'll be at Harrah's playing poker if you need me."

"Okay, Dad. We'll speak soon, I'm sure."

"Love you, Son."

"Me too, Dad."

The rest of the day is quiet...business as usual, mostly finalizing a few details for the new club. Just as I'm about to call it a day, Patrice walks in looking like herself again.

"You're alive," I say, laughing. "I was getting worried."

"Then why are you laughing?" she asks, laughing along with me.

"The look on your face this morning was classic, when you saw Bruce in my kitchen."

"Yeah, I about died," she says, burying her face in her hands. "How embarrassing!"

"I thought it was hilarious, actually."

"Yep, hilarious. So, he told me that you guys worked everything out. I'm happy to hear that."

"We did, and now I can move forward with everything here with a clear conscience."

"I'm really happy about that, for both of you," she replies, smiling. "Hey, is Dawn here? I could've sworn I heard her voice down the hall when I was walking to the elevator."

"She is," I reply, nodding. "That girl has the loudest voice...I can't believe that she isn't Italian."

"Seriously," she says, laughing.

"Speaking of Dawn, we are taking her out to dinner tonight. Welcome her to Las Vegas in style."

"Oh no. Count me out. I was welcomed enough last night."

"You're going, Patrice. Not up for discussion," I say, giving her my most serious stare.

"And if I don't go? Are you going to fire me, finally?"

"Yes."

"You are such an ass."

"I know. Now go upstairs and put on something nice. I'm taking you girls some place fancy."

"Fancy, huh?" Patrice says, perking up a bit now.

"Actually, I'll walk with you. I need a shower myself."

"I was gonna say something…" she teases as she pinches her nose.

"Don't start, and check on Dawn, would you? Make sure she's getting ready."

"Yes sire, I'm on it."

While waiting in the lobby for the girls, I receive an email from Scarlett. Apparently I didn't send a strong enough message yesterday, and am still uninterested in anything else she has to say. So, I hit delete before tucking my cell safely away into the pocket of my suit coat to be ignored for the night, remaining blissfully ignorant for just awhile longer.

"Do you approve, sire? Is this fancy enough?" Patrice asks as she does a little twirl.

"I do, and yes it is," I reply, nodding. "You look beautiful." Trying hard not to over-check her out, I get up from the couch and fasten the button my coat.

"Not too bad yourself there, Donnie."

"I shaved," I reply with a wink.

"Oooh, I love your dress!" Patrice says, beaming as Dawn joins us, and the two embrace, gushing over how great they both look.

After a painful few minutes of jewelry and makeup discussions, and endless compliments, I interrupt, explaining that we have a reservation at FiAMMA in thirty minutes.

"Seriously, Donnie? FiAMMA?" Patrice asks.

"Yes, seriously, and we had better get moving, ladies," I reply, escorting them out the door, and into the black stretch limousine that is waiting out front.

"Okay, now I'm feeling spoiled! A limo, boss?" Dawn is wide-eyed and beaming as she gets in.

"I've been dying to go there forever, Donnie. I'm so excited!" Patrice says, getting into the limo behind Dawn.

"It's good?" Dawn asks.

"Better than good, Dawn," I answer with a nod. "And I must say, you're looking extremely beautiful tonight yourself. I've only seen you dressed up once or twice."

"Yeah, at Lily's wedding, I think. I do look good, huh?" she boasts, laughing.

"You look good," I answer, chuckling as I settle into the leather seat, shaking my head.

"Thanks, Donovan. You kinda wanna hit on me right now, huh?" she says with a wink.

"Oh, absolutely, Dawn," I answer, returning a teasing wink.

"I knew it," she says, laughing.

"Anyway…" Patrice interrupts, rolling her eyes.

We arrive at the MGM Grand and make our way to FiAMMA, and are seated almost immediately. After looking over the wine list, I choose a bottle of *Castello di Ama, L'Apparita*, asking the waiter for more time before we order.

"This place is so elegant," Patrice says, taking in the warm ambiance of the restaurant.

The finest china, white linen tablecloths, low lighting, and soft music set the scene for the most romantic of dates, which, in this threesome, we are not a part of...not that I would complain.

"I know, right?' Dawn adds. "And would you look at this menu? I'm ordering one of everything."

"I've seen you put it away, Dawn, but I highly doubt that you could eat one of everything," I reply, laughing. "But order whatever you like, both of you."

As we finish our meals, my cell begins vibrating in my coat pocket. Beeping once, twice, and now thrice, to the point of aggravation...forcing me to give in and pay attention to it. I'm thankful to see Jared's name and not hers.

"It isn't…?" Patrice asks, giving me that *oh shit* stare.

"No, it's Jared, actually. He decided to come early as well, and wants to know where we are."

"Okay, good," Patrice says, relieved.

"Jared is here?" Dawn asks, suddenly perking up.

"He is, and wants us to meet him at the Sky Lounge."

"Oh no! Count me out…" Patrice says, shaking her head in disgust.

"Stop it. You are absolutely coming," I interrupt.

"Come on Patrice, it'll be fun!" Dawn adds.

"Seriously, guys. I'm not up for it."

"I told him that we'll be there in thirty minutes. Dessert anyone?"

"I hate you," Patrice says, trying to hide a smile.

"I know." I nod.

Eleven

...What's wrong with you? Were you dropped on your head as a baby?

P.A.

“I'm am not drinking that,” Patrice says, wrinkling her nose as I push a shot in front of her.

“Just one...hair of the dog, Patrice. You'll feel better, trust me,” I explain.

“I'll drink it,” Jared says, reaching for the shot glass.

“Fine, jeez! I’ll drink it, assholes...” Patrice grunts, picking up the glass, quickly tossing it back.

“A toast to us,” Dawn says, holding up her shot glass... “The Vegas crew!”

Patrice glares at me while slamming her glass down on the table, while Dawn and Jared hit the dance floor. The music is loud, and the strobe lights overhead are pulsing flashes of light. My repeated attempts to get Patrice on the floor fail, so we sit and watch everyone else enjoying themselves.

“Go ask someone to dance, Donnie. I don't mind.”

“I'm not about to leave you here alone wearing that dress,” I say, trying hard once again not to stare.

“I'm a big girl, I'll be fine,” she replies rolling her eyes at me.

“I don't think so…”

Dawn and Jared have become that sweaty, grinding couple that nobody wants to see...the *get-a-room* couple. I've never seen them flirt at this level, and am beginning to wonder if both of them showing up early today was, in fact, a coincidence.

"What's going on there?" Patrice asks, watching Jared and Dawn with a confused look.

"How would I know? You and Dawn are in charge of Gossip Central, not me."

"True, but she's never said anything to me about liking him."

"Well, he passed me a note in biology the other day and told me that he had a crush on her," I say, teasing.

"Why do you always have to be such a dick?" she says laughing.

"The obvious answer here would be, because I can, but I'll refrain from saying that."

"Jesus, Donovan. You love to push my buttons, don't you?"

"Actually, yes. This is the most fun I've had all week," I reply, laughing.

"Yeah, it's not so fun for me, you know."

"Yes it is."

"No, it's really not," she says, hiding a smile.

"Then tell me, Patrice, what would be fun for you?"

"Oh, maybe a week on some remote beach," she replies, staring off into space. "Maybe Hawaii."

"So, go then."

"I can't. My boss is a dick, and won't let me off for an entire week."

"Then quit."

"Shut up."

"Patrice, take a fucking vacation. I have never and would never stop you."

"I know, and I'm sorry I'm being such a bitch. I don't know what's going on with me."

"I do," I reply, looking away as I take a sip of my drink.

"Oh really? Do tell."

"And get punched? No thank you," I say, laughing.

"Seriously, I wanna know."

"Patrice," I say, leaning in, resting my elbows on the table. "Can you even remember the last time that you had a really good deep dicking?" I move back, trying hard not to laugh.

"Deep dicking? What's wrong with you? Were you dropped on your head as a baby?"

"Come on, you know that was funny, and I'm just trying to loosen you up, make you laugh. You are wound up extra-tight tonight."

"No I'm not, and you seem to have forgotten that I just spent half the day sick as hell."

"You're absolutely right, I apologize, Patrice. Would you like to leave?"

"No, I don't want to spoil the evening for everyone," she says, glancing at the dance floor, watching as Jared and Dawn grind away on each other.

"I will take that as a yes." I get up and walk out to the dance floor to let Jared and Dawn know that I'm taking Patrice back to Pisa, and that I'll leave them the limo. I collect Patrice, leave the club, and grab us a cab.

During the short ride back to, well, home, other than Patrice thanking me for a wonderful night, and apologizing for being such a buzzkill, we don't talk. I'm not really sure if she's just tired, or if she's actually mad at me for my deep dicking comment, but never being one to want to uncork a woman's innermost thoughts or unleash the demon, I stay silent myself.

"I'm not really all that tired...wanna come up for a cup of coffee?" Patrice asks.

"Coffee? Code word for deep dicking?" I ask, laughing.

"Dream on, Donnie...coffee means coffee," she says, shaking her head.

"Whatever you say, and sure."

Now in Patrice's suite, coffee brewing, television on, she flips the channels until she finds a movie.

"Is this okay?" she asks, settling on some old Steve Martin movie.

"Whatever you want to watch is fine," I answer, not really caring.

"I like him, he's funny," she says, eyes closing already.

"Not tired, huh?" I ask, laughing.

"No, just closing my eyes for a minute...waiting for the coffee to be done."

"I can go."

"No don't. I'd like some company."

"Alright," I say, kicking off my shoes, making myself comfortable. It begins to rain, and we can hear the drops become louder as they beat against the window, quickly turning into a full-blown thunderstorm. Before the coffee is ready, we both fall asleep on the couch.

"What the hell?" Patrice says, startled by a loud pounding on the door, rubbing her eyes.

"Are you expecting company?" I ask, smirking as I glance at my watch. "It's three-thirty in the morning. That sounds like a booty call to me."

"Stop it. I don't even know anyone here," she says, annoyed.

"Let me answer it. Maybe someone is trying to find me."

And, guess who? Scarlett is standing there, dripping wet, crying, smelling of cheap boxed wine...her favorite. She pushes past me and barges into the living room, glaring at Patrice, then back at me.

"I fucking knew it! Has this been going on the whole time?" she asks, yelling loud enough to wake the dead. "Well, has it? This is the second time I've found you two together!"

"Calm down, Scarlett. Nothing is going on," Patrice quickly says.

"You have to get ahold of yourself," I add. "What are you doing here?"

"You keep ignoring me. My calls, my texts, all of my emails. I'm sick of it, I don't deserve this shit!" she says, sitting on the couch, crying into her hands.

"I disagree, but here we are. The floor is yours, Scarlett," I say.

Patrice attempts to slip out of the room, and I tell her to stay. I may need witnesses.

"No, not until she leaves," Scarlett says, wiping her nose with her sleeve.

"The only one that will be leaving is you," I say, firmly. "This is your one and only chance to talk, and I suggest that you take it."

"Donovan, please. Let's just go to your penthouse and talk. You owe me that much."

"I owe you nothing, and I'm really growing tired of your bullshit, Scarlett. Now, this is your last chance to explain, so start talking, or get the fuck out."

"Why are you being so mean?" she asks, tears streaming down her cheeks.

"Oh, I'm sorry. Am I being mean to the girl who left me standing at the altar...twice? Please, tell me how I can fix things for you," I snarl.

"Donovan, I'm pregnant!" she says, shouting loud enough for all of Las Vegas to hear.

The room goes silent. Pins drop and no one hears them. My head begins to spin at her confession, and Patrice looks gutted. Not what I expected…

"Say something!" she cries out.

"I don't even know how to react. I think that you'd say anything to fix this at this point." *Unfuckingbelievable. Am I really supposed to buy this shit?* "And you're drinking?"

"I don't believe you, Scarlett," Patrice jumps in, yelling... "You really don't expect him to buy this crap, do you?"

"I do find it funny that you kept this from me, but feel the need to tell me now, after you've fucked everything up again," I add.

"It's *true*, I swear. I took a test," Scarlett says, looking down, crying...still crying.

"Yeah, okay, Scarlett," Patrice says, rolling her eyes. "You'd say anything right now to get him back. Donovan is right, you are grasping at straws."

Not wanting to gang up on her, but wanting to get to the bottom of this, I ask Patrice to give us a few minutes. After she leaves the room, I sit down on the opposite end of the couch from Scarlett, taking a deep breath, attempting to calm down and talk this through.

"Donovan, this is why I ran again. I was so scared of how you'd react because I know you're not ready to start a family yet. I didn't know how to tell you."

More crying, more excuses, more bullshit.

"This isn't the same as say, crashing my car, or spending too much at the mall. This is a baby, Scarlett. You don't keep shit like this from me."

"I know...and I'm sorry. I was just so scared."

"Alright, you were scared, you covered that. Now, let me ask you this...Is it mine?"

"What? Why would you ask that?" she asks, getting up from the couch, facing me. "Of all the shitty things you could say, that was the worst!"

"Why else would you be so scared to tell me, Scarlett? You didn't trust me enough to know that I would be able to handle this news, so I can only assume…"

"Stop saying that. It's yours, you asshole!" Crying...and more crying.

I'm finding it really hard to have any sympathy for her, though. My brain is on overload, and I need time to sort this shit out.

"Alright, then...tomorrow we'll go to the doctor together and get a pregnancy test. And you can be sure that I will be demanding a paternity test."

"Fuck you, Donovan. I don't need this shit, especially not right now!" she says, storming out.

"Meet me out front in the morning, ten o'clock sharp! And lay off the booze would you?" I shout as she runs crying down the corridor. I slam the door and walk in the direction of the refrigerator in search a beer.

Upon hearing the door slam, Patrice decides that it's safe to come out from hiding, and joins me in the kitchen. Both of us speechless, she, too, grabs a beer, and together we stand in her kitchen in the silence.

Twelve

... I'm not lettin' you outta here until you've tasted my pie, Sugar.

Rockin' Robin

The doctor has confirmed the news, sadly, to be true, and after dropping Scarlett off at her budget hotel, I take one of my head-clearing drives. Only this time, I have the sandy dry desert of Nevada as my backdrop, as opposed to the sandy beaches of Southern California, and the calming view of waves crashing on the beach that I've become so accustomed to.

No, this is not the ideal situation to bring a baby into. This is not how I planned on starting a family. And life rarely seems to care about what our perfect plans seem to be.

I will say this...a baby will not bring Scarlett and I back together as a couple. As parents, yes, but I don't...can't...and will never trust that girl again.

That said, at this point, I question her ability to even be a mother right now. She has proven herself to be unstable more than once.

I certainly can pick ‘em.

A call comes in just as I'm pulling into a gas station. Relieved to see Patrice's name come up on the screen, I answer.

“What's up, Patrice?”

“So, what happened at the doctor's?” she asks, worry in her voice.

“She's definitely pregnant.”

“Shit!” It becomes quiet on the phone for a minute, she's probably in shock. “I'm so sorry, Donovan.”

Insert even more awkward silence here, neither of us knowing what to say regarding said hot fucking mess.

"Where are you?" she asks.

"About thirty minutes outside of Las Vegas, in Paradise," I reply.

How ironic. I am in hell, and getting gas in a town called Paradise.

"Find a coffee shop or something and text me the address. I'm coming to you."

And before I can answer, the call drops.

Forty minutes later, Patrice meets me at *Rockin' Robin's Diner & Pie Shoppe.* As you can imagine, it's a fifties-themed diner complete with a black-and-white checkered floor, old 45's plastered across every wall, and poodle skirts for miles. An old jukebox appropriately plays *Jailhouse Rock*, which is to become the anthem for my life, knowing that I will be doing hard time with Scarlett for at least the next eighteen years.

"This place is so cute," Patrice says as she joins me in a booth.

"It looks like the kind of place my dad would like," I answer, gesturing to the waitress to come over.

"Yeah, he would love it here," Patrice agrees as she looks around the colorful diner.

"Have y'all eaten here before?" the waitress asks, smiling as she grabs the pen nestled behind her ear.

"We haven't," Patrice answers, returning a warm smile.

"Well, why not? I only make the best pies in all of Nevada," she says with a wink.

"Oh, you're Rockin' Robin?" Patrice asks, laughing.

"The one and only, darlin'," she says as she points to her name tag. "So what can I get y'all?"

"Just coffee for me," I say, pushing the menu aside.

"Oh no, I'm not lettin' you out of here until you've tasted my pie, sugar," Rockin' Robin says as she shoots me a playful wink. "Now, you look like a key lime pie man. Am I right?"

"Sure," I reply laughing. "That sounds good."

"I knew it," she replies with a wink before turning to Patrice. "And for you, darlin'?"

"That does sound good. I'll have the same."

"You got it, sweetie. I'll get that right out with some nice hot coffee." And off she goes, swinging her hips in a crazy pink poodle skirt and singing about a hound dog along with the jukebox.

"She's fun," Patrice says, laughing.

I nod in agreement, not feeling up to talking, having fun, or eating pie, which I am always up for. And before I stray off-topic, I muster up a few words to snap myself out of this Scarlett-induced coma.

"Maybe you should get a job here. I saw a Help Wanted sign in the window."

"Not so fast, pal. I came here to talk about this whole baby situation," Patrice says in a very serious, not-taking-your-shit-today-Donnie voice.

"I understand, but, what is there really to discuss? I've already demanded a paternity test, and if it is in fact mine, I will do the right thing."

"And what? Marry her?"

"Fuck no. I will take care of my kid."

"Okay, jeez. Give me a heart attack why don't you?" Patrice says, shaking her head.

"I may be stupid, but I am not insane."

"Donovan, you're the farthest thing from stupid. You loved her...very much, by the way...and you did what anyone else in love would do...you gave her a second chance."

"Because I'm stupid...or just a glutton for punishment," I reply, shrugging my shoulders.

Saved by the pie. Robin delivers two slices of mile-high-key-lime-pie, as she calls it, accompanied by two cups of hot coffee. I dive right in, deciding that filling my mouth with the tasty pie will keep me from having to discuss this nightmare of a situation any further.

“Mmm, so good…” Patrice mumbles, mouth full of pie.

“Mhmm…” I eat, and I nod. Just as long as I don't have to talk.

I think that Patrice has sensed my reluctance to carry on this conversation, so we sit together in silence, both concentrating on the mile-high limey deliciousness.

Don't get me wrong...I know that this topic is far from dead, but a little quiet right now is one hundred percent necessary.

“Alright, enough of this, Donnie,” Patrice exclaims, wiping her mouth before standing up. “Come on,” she continues, holding out her hand. “We need to just blow this off and go have some fun!”

“I'm not really in the mood for…”

“Well, I don't really care what you're in the mood for, Mr. Crabby Ass,” she quickly interrupts. “Get up...!”

Bossy Patrice is a little scary, I have to admit. I barely get the chance to drop a twenty on the table before she is dragging me out of the cafe.

“Where are you taking me?” I ask as she drags me down the sidewalk.

"You'll see."

We cross the street and land at a run-down old movie theater. Displayed in mostly missing letters, the faded and cracked marquee reads,

ARL E CHA LIN
in
"TH GREAT D CTA OR"

"What the fuck is that supposed to say? This place looks like it went out of business a few decades ago," I say, finally cracking a smile.

"Oh stop it. Clearly it says, Charlie Chaplin in The Great Dictator," she says as she points at the marquee. "Get your eyes checked, old man."

"Chaplin? This is a silent film?" I ask, already knowing the answer.

"You'll do what I say, and you will like it," she says, interrupting yet again. "And, for your information, this is his first film with dialogue, so no more excuses," she replies, rolling her eyes. "Now let's go in."

"Fine," I say, shaking my head. "I could use a nap."

Thirteen

...Yeah, but I'm not waiting around forever though, buddy.

Kelein

The not-so-silent film was, if anything, a great escape. Aside from Patrice nudging me every fifteen minutes to wake up, I enjoyed the break from my current reality.

Back at Pisa, it's business as usual. With work being the only form of sanity for me right now, I spend the week focusing on the new club. Permits are in place and renovations are almost complete. Now all that needs to be done is to plan the grand opening.

"Patrice, I need to see you in my office," I say into the office intercom.

"Right away, sire," she replies, ever the smartass.

She joins me in my office, fresh cup of coffee in hand, and quickly takes a seat before setting the cup down on my desk. She begins to talk, but I don't seem to hear a word she says. Instead, I get lost in the steam rising from the coffee cup. Who am I kidding? My thoughts are not on business...they are on *Scarlett.*

"Donnie?" Patrice says as she snaps her fingers at me. "Hello?"

"I'm sorry. Where were we?"

"We were nowhere. You seem to be somewhere else," she says, concerned. "What's going on with you?"

"Oh, I don't know. My ex-fiancé is pregnant...probably with someone else's kid."

"You don't know that," she says, shaking her head. "Listen, I'm not defending her, but maybe you need to sit down and talk to the poor girl...give her a chance to explain, and…"

"Explain what?" I interrupt.

"Come on, Donnie, I know you very well, maybe better than anyone. You really don't expect me to believe that you can just walk away from all of this, do you? I mean, if a baby wasn't involved...sure, maybe. But she is pregnant, most likely with your child, whether you want to believe it or not. Just talk to her."

"We have work to do," I snap back, ignoring her rant.

"Fine, just trying to help. I'm staying out of it from now on," she says, snapping right back.

"Good. Now can we get to work?"

Talk about an uncomfortable afternoon…

Patrice is distant, to say the least...snappy, and at times...a bitch. It isn't often that you see her act like this, and let me tell you, the woman knows how to hold one hell of a grudge. But, she is right. She usually is. I do need to handle this situation and talk to Scarlett.

"Why don't we wrap this up for today, and we can pick it back up in the morning?" I say, shoving the notes for the opening into a folder. "Would you like to grab dinner?"

"No thank you, sir," she says, clearly still pissed. "If you're sure there isn't anything else, I'll be off."

“Patrice, come on. I’m sorry, please let…”

“Goodnight then, sir,” she interrupts with a curt nod. She turns, leaving the office, nose high in the air.

Christ. Note to self...don't piss off Patrice.

I switch off the lights in my office and just as I'm heading out, a face in the reception area that I recognize from the distant past greets me with a warm smile. Puzzled, I return the smile, and just as I'm about to ask if she needs help, she bails me out, revealing herself to me.

“Donovan, it’s me, Kelein.” she says, rolling her eyes. “You seriously don't remember?”

“Kelein, yes...of course,” I reply with a nod, still searching my memory. “How are you?”

“Please tell me you remember me.”

“From The Underground, right?” I do remember her, thank god. Bullet dodged.

“Yes,” she replies, seeming relieved.

“What brings you to Pisa?”

“You do, silly,” she says sort of seductively, as she flutters her lashes. “I couldn't believe it when I heard you left Malibu, so I came to see what happened.”

And you...basically a stranger...expect me to tell you the sordid details about my personal life... because...?

Trying not to appear annoyed and not wanting to be rude, I explain that I was just on my way out, and I ask her if we can catch up later. Kelein, not being one to take no for answer...as I now remember...asks if she can tag along. My brain is fried, and I am too tired to think, so I say yes.

"Cool! Where are we going?" she asks.

"I was just heading downstairs for a bite."

"That sounds great, but can we eat after?" she asks as she shuts the door to the reception area, and pushes me up against the wall as she starts to unbutton my shirt. "Let's finish what we started, Donovan. I want you to fuck me, right here, right now."

We begin to kiss, and for a moment I forget about Scarlett and the drama that comes with her. My hands begin to glide down Kelein's dangerous curves as I give in to her demands, tugging on her blouse and pulling it up over her head. The windows in the reception area start to fog up as things become more heated, but the sound of my zipper going down snaps me back to reality.

It wasn't the right time back then, and it certainly isn't the right time now. All of the Scarlett shit has me confused, not to mention emotionally drained. I suppose taking Kelein up on her offer could help me move on, but I'm not sure that I want to.

"Kelein, stop. I just can't do this," I say, taking a step back, pulling up my zipper.

“Stop? Don't do this to me again, Donovan,” she says, pleading.

“I am sorry, but this isn’t right,” I reply, retrieving her blouse from the floor, handing it to her. “My life is...complicated right now, and it wouldn't be fair to you.”

“I don't care, I just want to be with you. Use me, Donovan. Use every single inch of my body for your every desire,” she says breathlessly, as she presses her body back against mine.

“Kelein...no,” I reply, peeling her off of me. “As tempting as that offer is, I have shit to handle first.”

“And then we can?” she asks, her voice hopeful.

“Can I get back to you on that?” I reply, shooting her a wink.

“Yeah, but I'm not waiting around forever though, buddy.”

“Noted.”

“So, I'm gonna go,” she says, shrugging her shoulders, smiling. “But I won't stop trying.”

“Noted,” I reply, shooting her a facetious grin. “You never know, maybe next time...”

I escort her through the lobby toward the entrance of Pisa, and just as she rises up on her toes for a parting consolation kiss, I see Scarlett standing just outside, watching us.

Fourteen

...My life, much like his, will never be the same.

D.H.

And, by the look on her face I can see that she is really pissed.

Confused.

Gutted.

I think this might be the right time for that talk...

She joins me inside and before I can get a word out, she throws her arms around me and begins to sob. But this time her tears seem to be coming from a different place, a place of pain, regret, sorrow. This time her tears are not from anger, or even from fear. I can feel her body weaken as I wrap my arms around her. I can feel her heart beating against mine as I pull her closer. I can feel that suddenly, everything is different.

"Why don't we go upstairs and talk?" I ask.

She doesn't answer with words, only with a slight nod of her head. We walk hand in hand to the elevator in silence, both of us knowing that we are about to have a talk that will forever change both of our lives in one way or another.

I sit down on the couch in front of the fireplace, taking a deep breath, preparing myself for the worst...but as always, hoping for the best. This conversation could go in any direction, but it needs to happen, and it needs to happen now. She sits down next me, then relaxes back into the soft leather cushions of the couch. I watch her chest rise and fall a few times while she wrings her hands together trying to calm the obvious shaking. She swallows hard, taking a deep breath of her own before looking up, finally locking her eyes on mine.

"Donovan," she starts off, her voice soft and a little shaky, "...please let me get this out before you say anything."

"Of course...I'm listening," I answer with a slight nod.

"So, first I need to tell you that I'm not mad about you and that girl that I saw you with earlier. I brought it all on myself, and I practically pushed you into that...you know, being with someone else. I don't blame you, I blame me. I've fucked up over and over with you, and I don't deserve your forgiveness, but I'm asking for it. When I met you I was in a bad place, but I didn't want anyone to see that side of me, so I always pretended that everything was okay. I actually convinced myself that it was, but to be honest, my life was nothing but a lie. When you...this successful, handsome, incredible guy...actually wanted to be with me, I knew I had to work even harder at keeping up that pretense so you would never see the messed up me. Then when Ricardo found me, it all came to the surface, and I was scared. So scared that I ran...as you remember, and I knew...I just knew that you'd never want to be with that girl, that stupid girl who made a really bad decision and ruined her life. But when we got through all of that and you still loved me, I guess I became even more scared because I still felt that one day you'd wake up and ask yourself, 'what the hell am I thinking?' and just leave, and I couldn't take that kind of pain. Why would a guy like you want to be with a girl like me? So when you arranged that beautiful surprise in Venice, I freaked out again, and well...you know. I had just found out a week before that I was pregnant, and I didn't know how to tell you, or even if I would tell you, because for a fleeting moment I didn't know if I'd even keep it. But once again I messed everything up, and left you standing there, confused and wondering. I can't change anything that I've done, I can only try and fix it, and I promise you, Donovan, if you'll give me just one more chance, I swear that I'll make sure you don't regret it, not for a minute. We still have a chance to be a happy family, just like we've always dreamed we would be. So, I guess what I'm asking is, can you forgive me?"

The silence in the room is deafening as I take in everything that she has said. It isn't far off from her last apology, but this time I sense something different in her words. I sense a newfound strength in her owning up to those previous mistakes, and maybe a freedom...a break from that girl that she was, the one that doesn't know what it is to be loved. I take my time in responding, because I need for my answer to honest and true. This girl has beaten herself up enough, and I won't be adding to that. I see her in an entirely different light than I ever have, and fuck-ups aside, although they were big, she is still, and always will be my fate.

But...and yes, there is a but...this time things will be different, and I will make certain of that. This time we have a baby to consider, and that changes the entire game. I want to believe that she means every word that she said, but with anything aside from a voodoo cleansing ritual, I won't really be sure.

"Scarlett," I begin, moving closer to her on the couch and taking her hand in mine. "Have you forgotten that I already forgave you for the Ricardo situation? And, have you forgotten that I have already accepted everything about you and your past? I need for you to trust me, and to believe that I love you, no matter what. The running needs to stop. We have no chance of any kind of future if I can't trust that you won't run away every single time shit gets hard. If we are going to do this, then things need to be different, starting right now. You can't keep secrets from me because you're scared of the outcome, or afraid that I'll be mad at you. Do you understand what I'm saying?"

"I do," she replies with a nod. "And I do trust you, Donovan. I'm so sorry...for everything."

"You didn't really trust me, or you would have come to me, both times. Are you one hundred percent ready to change that now?" I ask.

"Yes, baby. A million percent ready. I'll never keep anything from you again, I promise."

"I am going to hold you to that, you know," I say before moving in for a quick, yet passionate kiss.

"I know, and thank you...thank you for believing in me, and for loving me like you do." She pulls me into another kiss, deeper this time, and it's as if we are both transported back to the beginning. Back to the first kiss we ever shared, back when things were brand new and uncomplicated. She pulls away, and looks into my eyes with a serious, yet playful stare. "So, you forgive me?"

"On one condition..." I reply with a smirk.

"Anything, Donovan."

Her eyes are bright and full of optimism as she anticipates my response. This is one of those rare moments when Scarlett is actually speechless and waiting with...well...bated breath, for lack of a better term. But, without any digressing to be seen, I move in for the kill.

"Anything?" I ask.

"Yes, Donovan. Just tell me what I need to do to fix this."

"You, my sweet girl, need to marry me, and not leave me at the fucking altar again."

"So, when in Vegas?" she replies, relieved that my request wasn't something more of the you-need-therapy sort of thing.

"My thoughts exactly," I answer, grinning.

"It has to be something outrageous, don't you think?"

"I do think," I reply, laughing. "And by the way, I mean now."

"Like, right now?" she asks, her luminous smile now spread from ear to ear. "Should we get Patrice, Dawn, and Jared at least?"

"No, just you and me, beautiful."

"Okay, but can I change first?" she asks, laughing, looking down at her faded jeans.

"No, but I will take you to any store in Vegas and buy you whatever you like."

"Okay," she says, and we both get up at the same time, meeting in the middle of the living room for a kiss to seal the deal.

"Donovan, thank you for believing in me...for forgiving me."

"Scarlett, when will you get it through your hard head that you are everything I've ever wanted? I love you. I always will, and nothing you can do will ever change that."

"You're so sappy, baby," she says playfully.

"I know."

And we're off. Off to drop a lot of money in some over-priced Las Vegas boutique. We make it down the elevator and through the lobby before our bubble of bliss is threatened by a scowling Patrice, who apparently saw us coming off the elevator, hand in hand, kissing, and laughing.

"Well, isn't this a pretty picture? So it looks like you two made up..."

"Yes, isn't it wonderful?" Scarlett says, unaware of Patrice's obvious snarky sarcasm.

"Not now, Patrice. We are on our way out," I say.

"To get married!" Scarlett says, giggling as she gives my hand a squeeze.

"Seriously? Don't you think you should wait a minute...see if everything actually works out this time?" she says, glaring right in Scarlett's direction.

"Patrice, everything has been sorted out between us, and I will explain it all to you tomorrow. Capisce?" I say through gritted teeth as I pull on Scarlett's hand, trying to make an escape, not wanting to deal with Patrice at the moment.

"This is too fast, and you know it, Donnie. You know how she can be," she says, her brow furrowed, her voice full of worry.

"Tomorrow, Patrice!" I snap back.

Scarlett and I keep moving toward the doors of Pisa, but are stopped in our tracks one last time as she continues.

"Donovan...I'm sorry, but I think you're making a mistake," she says, the volume of her voice rising slightly.

I turn to Scarlett and kiss her quickly on the cheek. "Let me handle this, baby girl."

Taking Patrice aside and out of ear-range of everyone, I attempt a quick explanation. "Listen, I know this makes no sense to you, but at your suggestion, I had a long talk with her, and you need to trust that I know what I'm doing."

"Donovan, she's left you standing alone at the altar twice...or have you forgotten that tiny piece of information?"

"No, Patrice, I haven't. But you know me well enough to know that I would never make the same mistake twice...well, thrice..." I say, chuckling.

"No, I know that, but I'm just worried about you. I don't want to see you get hurt again...you know, hurt thrice..." she says, laughing with me, pulling me into a tight hug. "I love you, Donnie, and she has always been what you wanted, so go...go marry your girl."

"Thank you, Patrice," I reply, nodding.

And as we pull away we look deep into each other's eyes, holding the gaze with no words spoken. At that moment, we both know that everything is going to be alright. Patrice does know me, better than anyone, and she is right, Scarlett has always been what I wanted. I give Patrice another quick hug, and return to my girl.

"Ready to go?" I ask Scarlett, taking her hand, walking toward the door.

"No," she says, stopping me. "Baby, I messed up the first two weddings, and I want this one to be perfect. Go get Patrice, Dawn and Jared. I want the people who are special to you to be there. Then, call your dad, and have them meet us at La Fuga."

"You don't want to get married here?"

"No, I want to get married on the beach, where you grew up, in Malibu," she says, smiling before calling Patrice over.

"Change of plans, Patrice...we need your help."

"What's going on?" Patrice asks, looking at us with utter confusion.

"Ask her," I say, looking at Scarlett, laughing. "She's the boss."

"Will you find someone to officiate the wedding, and get everyone together?"

"Of course I can, Scarlett. When and where?" she asks.

"Tomorrow morning, say...eleven, at La Fuga."

"Done and done," Patrice says, pulling Scarlett into a hug. "And I'm sorry for being such a bitch, you know...the other day."

"I deserved it," Scarlett says. "And I was the bitch. You were just being a good friend to Donovan."

"Alright, ladies," I interrupt. "We have a plan then?" I ask, laughing.

"We have a plan, baby," Scarlett says, grinning from ear to ear.

"Let's do this then!" Patrice says, smiling. "You guys go, and I'll get everyone there. I'll handle everything."

"Thank you for doing this, Patrice," I say, giving her a tight hug before we leave. "And, I love you too."

"So, we're Malibu bound?" I ask Scarlett as we walk to my car.

"That's right. Cool with you?"

"Yes," I reply, laughing. "Cool with me."

We've been on the road for about an hour, and as you can imagine, both of our cell phones are going off nonstop. The ceremony has been moved to sunset, which I would've suggested in the first place if Scarlett would've let me get a word in, but I had no intention of interrupting the conversation between her and Patrice for anything.

"Baby, I haven't eaten all day. Can we stop soon?"

"Of course. I think there's a few places coming up soon." I grab her hand and bring it to my lips. It never ceases to amaze me how things can go from complete shit to complete bliss in so little time. Life is pretty damn good at the moment.

We pull off the highway, settling for a truck stop. It isn't my first choice, but Scarlett has just told me that she was about to die from starvation, so a truck stop it is. Greasy cheeseburgers and fries seem to be the safest bet, so we order and discuss wedding details.

"We still need to get you a dress, baby girl," I say in between bites.

"I still have my wedding dress."

"Alright, unless you want something new. That's up to you."

"What about for you? We need to rent a tuxedo."

"I was thinking of something more casual. Who wears a tuxedo for a beach wedding?"

"I don't know. Anybody who wants to, I guess," she replies, laughing.

"What would you like me to wear?"

"It doesn't matter to me, you could wear shorts and I'd be happy."

"Works for me."

"Okay, I was kidding," she says, still laughing. "How about a nice button-down shirt, no tie, nice slacks?"

"I can do that," I reply, smiling, relieved not to hear the word tuxedo.

"Okay, good. And since were going in a more causal direction, I'll get a simpler dress."

"What about your wedding dress?"

"New start, new dress?"

"Makes sense, baby. So, we're going shopping," I say, giving her a wink.

"And you know I hate to shop," she replies, laughing.

"Well, I don't want to force you."

"Oh, I'll manage somehow, baby," she says, returning a playful wink.

Now back on the road with indigestion, Scarlett plans the shopping excursion that will take place in the morning. I glance over at the paper smoothed out on her thigh as she makes a list, and throw in a few items of my own to add, namely the alcohol.

"I don't see a cake on that list," I add.

“Baby, there's no time to order a cake,” she says, trying hard to hide her disappointment.

“Call Lily. She can put something together by tomorrow.”

“Oh yeah! Why didn't I think of her?” she says, relieved as she dials Lily's cell.

My cell is blowing up with texts from my dad, Patrice, and Reggie. I scan the messages, but don't answer. They'll have to wait until we stop again but Dad’s says *Congrats, again*...and yes, he put *again* in quotations. Patrice has nailed down an officiant and will meet us at La Fuga in the morning, and Reggie asked if he could bring his new lady.

“Lily said that she'll take care of the cake, baby,” she says, smiling, obviously relieved. “I'm going to close my eyes, okay?”

“Sure, beautiful. I'll wake you up when we get to La Fuga.”

“Baby, wake up. It's our wedding day,” Scarlett says, well... *whispers*, actually, in my ear.

“Five more minutes,” I reply, not ready to open my eyes yet.

“You can take ten more minutes if you want, but I have to get in the shower. I'm meeting Patrice in an hour to get dresses,” she says, throwing the covers back, getting out of bed.

"I will need more than ten minutes, beautiful." I smirk, quickly pulling her back under the covers before climbing on top of her.

"I don't have time," she says, laughing as she attempts to push me off.

"Patrice will understand," I reply between kisses as I make my way down her naked body.

"Mmm, Patrice who?" she asks, giggling that giggle that I've missed so much.

She finally surrenders as I make a not-so-quick stop at my favorite place on her entire body. I bury my face between her legs, making sure not to miss a drop of her sweet, heavenly juices. She squirms, moans, and begs for more, as long as it's no longer than ten minutes.

"Baby, I'm going to be late," she says in between cries of hurried ecstasy.

"Sshhh..."

I ignore her and continue on my quest. Moving up to her lips, I kiss her hard as I slide my painfully hard cock inside her. I didn't realize until this moment just how long it had actually been since we had sex, any kind of sex. And now that I've become aware of that sad fact, I realize that ten minutes will probably be sufficient...

Dammit, I was right, and now I will digress.

"Baby, that was amazing," she says, kissing my lips one last time before getting up.

"It is what it is...and that was all your fault, you know," I reply, grumbling.

"And that usually doesn't happen, I get it… Now, I'm taking a shower. Do you and your blue balls want to join me?"

"You know they aren't actually blue anymore, right?"

"I know," she replies, laughing. "I get how balls work."

"Then promise me, future wife, that you will take care of my balls till death do us part," I say, somewhat seriously, yet laughing.

"Your balls will always be safe with me. That I promise you, baby," she replies, winking.

We get into the shower, both of us cracking up at the ridiculous, yet necessary conversation about my balls.

"Should I put something about this in my vows?" she asks.

"I dare you..." I reply.

"Here's my credit card," I say, handing her the card as we walk to the elevator.

"I've got mine, baby. That's okay..."

"Not up for discussion," I abruptly interrupt. "Take it."

"Thanks, my generous future hubby," she says, grinning, slipping the card into her purse.

"You get yourself the prettiest dress you can find, alright?"

"I will," she says, nodding her head.

"And shoes...whatever you need."

"You sure?"

"I'm sure. Whatever you need."

Patrice meets us in the lobby, and after a brief exchange regarding the wedding arrangements, they take off, and I go off in the direction of the kitchen to find Lily.

"How is the cake coming along?" I ask, finding Lily at the oven.

"Almost done, boss," she assures me. "Welcome back."

"Thank you. It's good to be back."

"Scarlett didn't give me much to go on, she just said to make something pretty."

"Just a simple cake, Lily. There will only be about fifteen of us, maybe twenty."

"That's what she said," she replies, nodding. "But I did make your favorite. Chocolate."

"Perfect, thank you."

"So, Patrice said to set everything up in the dining room. I have a case of champagne coming, and I did manage to throw some hors d'oeuvres together early this morning."

"Excellent! You're a lifesaver, Lils," I say, shooting her a wink. "It looks like you have everything under control here, so I am going to run a few errands of my own."

"Sounds like a plan, boss, and let me know if there's anything else I can do."

"I will. Thanks, Lils."

On my way out, I run into Dawn and Jared, who appear to be attached at the hip. I'm not surprised though, we all saw that one coming.

"Hey man, there you are. We've been looking for you," Jared says. "Can we do anything to help?

"Thanks, I think everything is under control, but check with Lily. See if she needs a hand in the kitchen," I say, nodding. "I'm actually on my way out to do a few things before tonight."

"Dawn," Jared says, "...see if Lily needs anything in the kitchen. I'll go with him, and we'll meet up before the ceremony."

"That was kinda bossy," she replies, laughing. "But, you go...I'll help Lily."

They kiss goodbye, lingering longer than anyone should when the boss is standing right there, but I ignore them and head for the door, with Jared quickly catching up.

"How's all of that going?" I ask.

"Oh yeah, that. It's good, real good, if you know what I mean," he replies, nudging me in my side.

"I know what you mean, but spare me the details right now. I have a lot to do before sunset."

"So, you don't want to hear how she's a freak in bed, or how she likes to su..."

"Nope, I don't want to hear about that. Not today...Not ever," I reply, shaking my head.

We take the Hummer down to the Malibu shops. First stop, Cartier. I choose the flat bangle platinum-and-diamond Love bracelet, paying extra to have it inscribed and ready in an hour.

Per Sempre Amore Mio, the inscription will read. Forever my love. Scarlett is my forever, and nothing will ever come between us again.

Next stop...something for me to wear. Shopping for myself is not my favorite thing to do, but Jared is something of a clothes guy, so he helps me choose the right outfit for tonight. With twenty minutes to spare, we leave the store and start walking in the direction of the next stop.

“Where next?” Jared asks.

“The travel agency. I need to book a honeymoon,” I reply. “It's just up the street.”

“Cool, cool,” he says with a nod. “Where are you taking her?”

“She has mentioned more than a few times that she's always wanted to go to the Bahamas.”

“Yeah, who doesn't wanna go to the Bahamas?” he says, laughing. “Good call, brother.”

While I'm finalizing everything with the travel agent, a call from Patrice comes in. I can hardly make out what she's saying, and take the call outside, assuring the agent that I'll be right back.

“Patrice, slow down. What's going on? I can hardly hear you,” I say, trying to hear over the sirens in the background.

“Donovan, you need to get to Cedars Sinai right away! Scarlett has been shot,” she informs me, barely able to get the words out, crying hysterically.

“Shot? By who? Patrice, slow down! What the fuck happened?” My adrenaline is pumping overtime, and my heart is beating out of my chest. I try to put her words together, while attempting to remain calm at the same time.

Fuck calm! This is my bride. “Tell me!” I yell into the phone.

"I'm sorry, Donnie. We were at 23rd Street Jewelry, and it got robbed right as we were paying, and security tried to stop them, then shots were fired...just get to the hospital, now, please!"

I motion to Jared to get his ass outside, now...then toss him the keys. With no explanation, I tell him to take us to Cedar Sinai. We run down the crowded sidewalk back to the Hummer, and with tires screeching, speed away.

"Jesus. We're leaving now, Patrice. Is she okay? Please tell me that she's going to be okay."

"She was hit by a ricochet bullet...on the side of her head, Donovan," she explains, still crying.

"Are you alright?" I ask, still trying to process all of this.

"I'm shaken up, but otherwise fine. An officer is taking me to the hospital right now, we're following the ambulance."

"Alright, we are almost there..."

I try my best to explain the situation to Jared, and as worried as I am, attempt to remain calm and as positive as humanly possible. I keep repeating to myself that she will be alright, she *has* to be alright.

Jared pulls into the hospital entrance, and with tires screeching, stops at the emergency room doors. I jump out of the Hummer, and run inside where I find Patrice, doubled over and crying, near the nurses station.

"Patrice, where is she?" I ask, my hands tremble as I pull her into a tight hug.

"Donovan..." she says as she pulls away, shaking her head before looking down at the floor. The silence that follows seems to last forever, and when she finally does look back up at me, she just shakes her head again repeating, *"I'm so sorry. I'm so sorry..."*

My legs instantly give out, and I drop to the floor. This can't be happening! I don't believe it. The world around me begins to spin, and all of the voices around me sound as if they are in a long echoing tunnel. Within minutes, I am surrounded by my dad and Shari, followed by Jared and Dawn, Lily, Reggie, and then Patrice. I hear nothing, I feel nothing. My stomach is in knots, and I can't breathe.

"Somebody get him some water!" I hear my dad yell, and almost instantly a bottle of water appears before me. I take a sip before dropping it to the floor. I am overcome with anger, confusion, and immense, incomprehensible pain.

I have no idea what to do right now.

After what seems like hours, I get up, and ignoring everyone, search for a doctor. I start at the nurses station, and in a complete daze, ask to speak to the doctor that saw her. I wait, watching my family and friends share in my grief as they comfort one another, but I choose to stay here, waiting for an answer.

"Mr. Hart," the voice approaching me says. "I'm Doctor Shaw, I saw Miss Montgomery when she came in. May I ask what your relation to the deceased is?"

The deceased. There it is...somebody finally said it out loud, making it true. I feel like a skyscraper has fallen on top of me and destroyed my world. I somehow find a way to answer him, but barely get the words out.

"I am her..." I pause to clear my throat, and choke back tears. "...*was* her fiancé. We were to be married in a few hours..."

"I see," he says, nodding. "Please accept my condolences, and if it is any consolation, she didn't suffer. Her CT scan showed..." and as he explains, my brain shuts off.

I can't hear a single word that he's saying. Any explanation that he has to offer isn't going to bring back my girl, and before he has finished explaining, I ask if I can see her.

"Yes, of course, Mr. Hart. We do need you to identify her body, since you are the closest thing to family here. Follow me."

I stop on the way to see Scarlett to ask Patrice to call her parents. I hand her my cell phone, telling her that the number is in my contacts. I then follow the doctor to a room where I find Scarlett covered up to her chin with a sheet. Her head is wrapped with layers of white gauze, but a spot soaked with her blood is visible on the right side. The doctor asks if I can identify the body, and I answer him saying that, yes, this is Scarlett Montgomery. He thanks me before leaving the room, but not before telling me that I may take a minute to say goodbye.

A minute to say goodbye. How will I ever say goodbye to her? I was just about to have a lifetime with her, and on the very day that we were finally going to make that lifelong commitment, I lose her. This time forever. How does one take *a minute to say goodbye?*

I sit here by her side holding her hand, and feel it beginning to turn cold. I tell her over and over how much I love her...how I don't know what I'll do without her, that I don't know how I can go on without her. I ramble on, talking about how she changed my life, and what her and the baby, and us being a family meant to me. Then it sinks in that I not only lost my girl today, but that I lost our child, too. I drop my head down on the mattress near her arm, and finally allow myself to cry.

My dad taps me on he shoulder, waking me up, and the first thing I notice is that it's dark outside. He explains that we have to leave and let them take Scarlett to the morgue.

"I fell asleep," I say, before leaning over Scarlett's body, placing a gentle kiss on her forehead. I take one last look at my beautiful girl before my dad leads me out of the room, and then, out of the hospital.

The drive back to La Fuga is reminiscent of the one that we shared when my mom died. An eerie silence. Only this time it is *me* who has lost his love. I understand now why my dad shut down and disappeared. My life, much like his, will never be the same.

Over the next few days, I find myself so busy with Scarlett's family in town...and the funeral arrangements...that I don't have time to sit around and feel sorry for myself. I'm grateful for that, actually, and grateful for the people that I have around me making sure that I get out of bed each day.

The day of the funeral has arrived, and I still can't believe that we are here. We gather at the cemetery to celebrate Scarlett's life, as her mother asked me to put it, as I begin to give my eulogy. I choke back tears as I talk about her, and share stories of our short time together, and talk about the future that we will never see together.

One by one, family and friends all speak with kindness and love about her, and tears flow with each and every word that is spoken. Single red roses are placed on her closed casket by everyone here, followed by a large bouquet of pink roses, her favorite, placed on top of the impressive pile.

We all stand together surrounding the casket, watching as they lower her body into the ground. There really isn't anyway to describe the gut-wrenching, horrible, empty feeling that you go through when you bury someone that you love. I'm not even going to try...

Following the burial is the customary get-together for cold cuts at a relative's house, but since her family lives out of state, we have it at La Fuga.

I don't want to sit around and talk about her. I don't want to hear stories about how cute she was when she was a little girl. I can't pretend for another second that I'm okay, much less another hour. I'm not okay, and I'm not sure if I ever will be.

Actually, what I'm thinking about right now is all the time that I wasted being angry at her for all of the stupid shit that she pulled, but it makes me smile at the same time, because if I didn't love her as much as I did, I would have never been mad. Funny. The person that you love the most can make you want to wring their necks, and at the same time you can't imagine a life without them. I suppose that's how it is when you learn to love someone unconditionally...warts, flaws and all.

As the cold-cut party begins to wrap up, one by one, family and friends make their way over to say their goodbyes before leaving to return to their normal lives. Everyone here will be forever affected in some way, but Scarlett's parents and I will have a hole in our hearts, and in our lives, always.

After dropping Scarlett's family off at the airport, I decide to drive somewhere just to be anywhere but here...a destination that will only be determined when I get there. But before I take off, I reply to a text from my dad who is worried about me. I let him know that I am taking off for a few days, and that I'm okay, whatever that means.

He replies simply with, *I'm here if you need me. I love you, son.*

I shut off my phone, and shut out the world. I pull onto Pacific Coast Highway, and begin to think about life, fate, and why I had to go through all of this only to end up alone and right back where I started. My inner dialogue is having the what-does-it-all-mean? discussion against my will. I turn on some music and drown out the voices.

A good Donovan-head-clearing-101 is in order. I don't know where I go from here, but wherever that is, Scarlett will always be right there watching over me...

I will love that girl until the day I die, and will forever be a changed man because of her.

Like I said...Fate is a funny thing.

Epilogue

...To my loving husband

Scarlett

I pull off the highway somewhere in Northern California for a bite to eat. Patrice had given me a letter at the funeral that Scarlett wrote to give to me after the wedding, along with a white gold ID bracelet with an inscription that read Forever Yours.

I've held off reading that letter until now, but after week on the road, I decide that I might be ready to handle it. I put on the bracelet, smiling at the inscription, and open the letter.

To my loving husband,
By the time you read this we will be married! I'm so proud to be your wife, and I promise to make you proud for choosing me, again, and again...and again.
You believed in me even when I didn't, and you loved me even when I didn't know how to love myself.
You, Donovan Hart, are my hero, and I will love and cherish you until the day I die.
Thank you for loving me, and thank you for marrying me.
Oh, and I promise to make sure that your balls never turn blue again!
We did it!
Your loving wife,
Mrs. Scarlett Hart

Fuck. Now I find myself back at square one, tearing up as I try to eat this ham and cheese sandwich. I fold the letter and place it safely in my back pocket. I probably won't read it again, but will cherish those words, her last words to me.

Just as I'm finishing up, Patrice calls for her daily check-in session. *How are you doing?* she asks. *Fine,* I answer. I tell her about the letter, and what it said. She asks where I am, and I tell her that I'm not really sure, but will ask. *Do you want me to come and hang out with you?* she asks. And as much as I've enjoyed being alone, I tell her yes, as long as she doesn't make me see a silent film this time. *Palo Alto,* I tell her, *but why don't we meet in Santa Barbara? I'll pack a bag,* she says, *and see you soon.*

Patrice, always to the rescue.

Time to rejoin the living. Who better than Patrice to help me do just that?

So, as they say, life goes on...and that, we know for sure.

Seven Months Later...

...here's to whatever the future holds.

Patrice

Feeling sorry for myself was never really my style. When my mom died, I did my best to pack that away, and I've done the same since Scarlett's untimely death. Now, before you jump to conclusions and think that I am some uncaring prick with no feelings, hold on. Losing her was devastating, it was. I lost my love. The one that was supposed to be with me until death do us part, but fate had other plans. So, instead of sitting around crying in my beer, I made the choice to move on with my life. I have no other choice.

I threw myself into the new club one-hundred-and-fifty-percent. I was fully immersed, and it kept my mind off of her...well, it helped.

So, here we are...seven months later, settled in Las Vegas, and the one thing that I can't seem to keep my mind off of is the fact that I'd be a father by now. Would I have made a good dad? Was it a boy or a girl? Would I have closed down the club because I had to be a responsible parent? Will asking myself these questions actually change anything?

Just turn the page...

“Donnie, it's time to get back out there,” Patrice says, serving up some stir fry sensation that she prepared for dinner.

“To what?” I ask, taking a bite of some tasteless slab of tofu. “What is this shit?”

“It's good for you, just eat it.”

“You sounded just like my mother right there, Patrice,” I reply, laughing.

“Fuck off, Donovan.”

“Settle down.” I drop my fork, and push my plate away. “I can't eat this shit, I need a cheeseburger.”

“Fine, you're right. It's shit,” she says, laughing as she piles her plate on top of mine. “In and Out?”

“Absolutely.” I nod.

“I can drive.”

And as we walk toward the door, I suggest that we just take off and go home for a few days. Pisa is under control, and I know Patrice could use a break...I know I need one.

“Yeah, okay. Let me pack a bag,” she says, walking off towards her room.

“Meet me in the lobby in an hour when you're done,” I say, chuckling.

“Ass, I'll be ten minutes,” she snaps back.

“Keep telling yourself that,” I reply as I leave her suite, going up to my penthouse to throw a few things into a bag.

We meet in the lobby three hours later. Okay, it was twenty minutes, and to be fair to Patrice, that was much faster than I expected.

The Hummer is loaded, and we’re off. First stop, food. We hit an In and Out before heading to Malibu. Patrice called dibs on the first CD of the trip. Yes, she actually said the word, dibs. Ed Sheeran begins the trip, and to be honest, this music makes me sleepy. I veto the dibs, and put in something a bit more upbeat.

“Come on, Donnie. That's my favorite CD!” Patrice exclaims, pouting.

“Sorry, I need to stay awake for four hours.”

“Then what's the point of dibs?” she asks.

“You started the whole calling-dibs thing, I don't have to go along with it, though.”

“It doesn't work that way. It's the same as calling shotgun,” she says, desperate to make her point.

“Alright, and who calls shotgun anymore?”

“Everybody.”

“Nobody,” I reply, laughing.

"Fine, but I get the next choice of music."

"What next? Tony Bennett?"

"Who?" she replies, laughing.

"Very funny. You know damn well that my dad played nothing but that, and Sinatra all day when he ran La Fuga."

"True, he did. But, no Bennett in my bag."

"Then what else do you have in there?" I ask, curious.

"Let's see," she says, digging through her oversized purse. "Madonna, Pink, Sheryl Crow..."

"Stop..." I interrupt. "No, no, and no to all of those."

"Why? What's wrong with them?"

"That's all chick music," I reply, shaking my head.

"Free your mind, Donnie. You just might like it."

"My mind is free, thank you. But not that free."

"Fine, I have this," she says, putting in another CD.

"What the fuck is that?" I ask.

"What? It's Nick Jonas."

I quickly swerve my Hummer to the side of the road, shaking my head and pointing out the passenger side window as I come to a full stop. "Get out of my car."

"Oh, stop it," she says, laughing. "Drive."

"Not with that playing, I won't." I remove the CD, toss it out the window shouting, outta my car! and pull away.

"What did you do that for?" she asks, looking out the back window for her CD in the road.

"Do I really need to answer that?" I reply, laughing.

"That was my favorite CD, Donovan."

"I'm sorry to hear that. I will replace it, alright. But that will never be played in my vehicle again."

"Sometimes you can be such a dick." She crosses her arms and begins to pout. I turn on the radio, and the next thirty minutes or so, we drive...no talking.

She finally fell asleep somewhere between Las Vegas and Malibu, and I took the opportunity to download the CD that I tossed onto her playlist. Hoping for redemption...

It feels good to be home. Nothing compares to the crisp ocean air, the smell of the ocean, and the sand under your feet. I instantly want a cold beer and a volleyball, but with everyone at work, I'll have to settle for the beer.

Just to recap, Bruce and Shari are pretty much the same, and La Fuga is thriving. The Underground is still there, but closed. Maybe my dad is holding onto it for me, knowing that the day will come when he retires and I will take everything over once again. Never say never, right?

After a long lunch with everyone at the hotel, I find myself alone walking along the shoreline, barefoot, waves crashing at my feet. I am thinking about her and about how much has changed in such a short time. I have spent the last several months in a rather pensive state, and, as I said before, it's time to let go of her, and think about what comes next.

"Donovan!" I hear a voice in the distance call out. Okay, I hear Patrice call my name...enough with the mystery here.

I turn to see her running to catch up, bright smile, slow-motion-like hair flowing in the wind. Not really, but it was fun to picture.

"Patrice, I thought you were going shopping?" I ask.

"I did," she answers, handing me a small jewelry box. "I picked this up from the jeweler's, she would want you to have it."

I instantly know what it is...the wedding present that Scarlett was picking out when she was killed. I'm not sure if I should be mad at Patrice, or if I should thank her for her thoughtful gesture. *Closure,* she explains, *and now you'll always have a piece of her with you.*

"Thank you," I say, choking on my words. "I'll open it later."

"Want to go to Nobu and get a beer?" she asks, quickly changing the subject as she senses my discomfort.

"That sounds good," I reply, nodding.

We continue walking until we reach the beachfront restaurant, finding two seats at the crowded outdoor lounge bar. I find myself eavesdropping on conversations around us in lieu of actually talking to Patrice. Not because I'm angry with her...just having mixed emotions at the moment, I suppose.

"Donnie, are you okay?" she asks.

"I am," I reply with a nod. "I just wasn't expecting that."

"She'd want you to have it."

"I know, and I appreciate it, Patrice. Thank you, again."

"You don't need to thank me. Like I said before, I hope it brings you some closure," she says, smiling.

I nod, not knowing what else to say, and to be honest, not wanting to continue the conversation.

"To whatever the future holds," she says, raising her glass of beer.

"To the future," I say, clinking my glass with hers.

"So, speaking of the future, Donnie. There's something I've been wanting to tell you...for a really long time, actually," she says, sort of reluctantly.

"Alright," I reply, intrigued.

She shifts uncomfortably on the bar stool, and I can sense an internal battle beginning within her. Deep breaths are taken, false starts of, *Um, I...* are on repeat.

*Christ...*what the hell has her so twisted up? Spit it out, woman.

"What is it, Patrice?" I ask, curiosity on the rise.

"Okay, here goes..." she begins, taking another pause and clearing her throat before forming an actual sentence. "Donovan, I'm in love with you," she blurts out, searching my eyes for a response. "I have been for awhile, and I just thought you should know."

My brain implodes from this new information, and I am unable to respond right away. She loves me? My friend, assistant, confidant? Unexpected? What?

Processing...

"Patrice..." I begin.

THE END

A Note from the Author

So, here we are at the end. I never expected to write one book, much less four. If I have learned one thing during this crazy joyride, it would be to never say never. Absolutely anything is possible if you just decide to do it. Cliché, but true.

Thank you for inspiring me through this experience, without you, and you know who you are, (my twitter ladies) I would have never been able to start, continue, or finish what I started.

I hope that I, if anything, have entertained you. Donovan, Scarlett, Patrice, and even that cheating whore Danielle gave me some pretty interesting stories to write for you.

Let's hope that Donovan is now living the life that he's always wanted. Madly, passionately in love and living in Venice, Italy? I hope so. He deserves it.

As always, I thank you for joining me, indulging me, and supporting me.

Much love,
Aj Linn

"Write drunk; edit sober."
-Hemingway

15618981R00100

Printed in Great Britain
by Amazon